A MESSAGE FROM
BEAR GRYLLS,
CHIEF SCOUT

Tiger Patrol is a team of intrepid Scouts who look out for each other no matter what challenge they face.

They've made a promise to do their best and this means picking up skills like navigation, planning, fire lighting and first aid. From moors and woodlands to river rapids, Tiger Patrol is willing to give anything a go – as long as they stay safe.

Scouting is full of great adventures, but you'll only make the most of them if you give everything you've got. You'll need to be alert, committed, trust your friends and never be too proud to ask for help.

Maybe you're already a Scout. If so – be inspired by Tiger Patrol. If you're thinking about joining, then go for it. I did, and I've never looked back.

Are you up for the challenge?

Survival Squad: the series

Available now:
Out of Bounds
Search and Rescue

Coming soon:
Night Riders

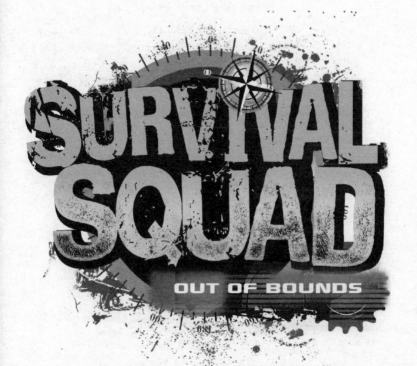

JONATHAN ROCK

RED FOX

With thanks to Paul May

SURVIVAL SQUAD: OUT OF BOUNDS
A RED FOX BOOK 978 1 862 30965 4

First published in Great Britain by Red Fox,
an imprint of Random House Children's Books
A Random House Group Company

This edition published 2012

1 3 5 7 9 10 8 6 4 2

The Random House Group Limited supports the Forest Stewardship Council
(FSC®), the leading international forest certification organization. Our books
carrying the FSC label are printed on FSC®-certified paper. FSC is the only
forest certification scheme endorsed by the leading environmental
organizations, including Greenpeace. Our paper procurement policy can be
found at www.randomhouse.co.uk/environment.

MIX
Paper from
responsible sources
FSC® C016897

Set in 13/19 pt Goudy by Falcon Oast Graphic Art Ltd.

Red Fox Books are published by Random House Children's Books,
61–63 Uxbridge Road, London W5 5SA

www.kidsatrandomhouse.co.uk
www.totallyrandombooks.co.uk
www.randomhouse.co.uk

Addresses for companies within The Random House Group Limited can be
found at: www.randomhouse.co.uk/offices.htm

THE RANDOM HOUSE GROUP Limited Reg. No. 954009

A CIP catalogue record for this book is available from the British Library.

Printed and bound in Great Britain by
CPI Group (UK) Ltd, Croydon, CR0 4YY

CHAPTER 1

Jay Watson looked on nervously as Lee rattled the temporary wire fencing that surrounded the building site.

'I reckon we can get in,' Lee said, glancing up and down the street. He wiped his hands on his faded red T-shirt, leaving a streak of dirt. 'Go on, Jay. There's no one around. Climb over and see if you can get the gate open from inside.'

'Yeah, go on, Jay,' Vicky urged him. 'You can do it, no trouble.'

Jay looked at the sign on the fence. 'There are guard dogs,' he said.

Vicky laughed. 'It always says that but I've never seen any.'

Jay sneaked a look at his watch, although he didn't really need to. It was starting to get dark.

He should have been home an hour ago.

'What are you waiting for?' asked Sean, Lee's mate.

'You're scared, aren't you?' Vicky taunted him, her face sneering in contempt. 'It's not just the dogs. You think someone's going to see you. You think you'll get in trouble.'

'No,' said Jay. 'It's not that.' He turned away from them, kicking the stones on the ground. He didn't want them to see that he was scared.

'What, then?' Lee demanded. 'I saw you looking at your watch. Is your mum going to tell you off for being late?'

'You're going to secondary school soon,' said Sean, 'with all of us. You can't let your mum tell you what to do all the time.'

The rest of the gang were older than Jay. When he started at the new school Lee would be in Year Nine and the others in Year Eight. He'd been flattered when they'd let him start to hang out with them, earlier in the holidays. But now he wasn't so sure.

'Well?' asked Lee unpleasantly.

Jay looked up to see his blue eyes staring hard at him. He hesitated.

'Forget it,' Lee said. He grabbed the fence and started to climb. 'Go home, saddo.'

Jay flushed. 'OK, then,' he said, grabbing Lee's leg. 'I'll do it. Get off.'

He was halfway up the fence when he heard laughter further down the street and saw two dark-haired boys and a girl with a blond ponytail walking towards them. They looked as if they were having fun, and Jay couldn't help wishing he was with them instead of with Lee and his gang.

'Hey, you lot!' Sean yelled suddenly. 'What's so funny? Are you laughing at us?'

The other kids glanced over at them, and then carried on walking.

'What's up with you, then?' called Vicky, leaping onto her bike and chasing after them. She jumped the kerb and skidded to a halt, blocking their way. 'My friend asked you a

3

question – don't you know it's rude not to answer questions?'

Lee grinned at Sean. 'Come on, this should be good.'

They ran across the road, laughing. 'Is she your girlfriend, then?' Sean said to the taller of the two boys.

'Yeah, come on,' said Vicky to the blonde girl, who was starting to look scared. 'Which one of them's your boyfriend? Tell us, and you can go.'

Jay jumped down from the fence. It was mean, what they were doing. Those kids had just been minding their own business. He knew he should tell the others to leave them alone, but right now he was just glad that they seemed to have forgotten about him. Maybe this would be a good time to get away. His bike was leaning against the wall of a nearby house and he started walking towards it, but suddenly one of the boys raised his voice.

'Just leave us alone, OK? We haven't done anything to you. Let us past.'

Jay saw Lee step forward, about to throw a

punch, but the smaller of the two boys put out a hand and pushed him away. The shove caught Lee off balance and he stepped backwards and crashed into Vicky, who yelled and let her bike fall to the ground. The blond girl shrieked as one of the pedals caught her leg, and suddenly everyone was shouting – and one voice was shouting louder than any of the others.

'Jasper Watson! What on earth do you think you're doing?'

Jay's heart sank as he heard the familiar voice call out to him. It was his mum.

She was standing on the pavement on the other side of the street, glaring at him, with her hands on her hips and her face flushed with anger. She'd been cooking and an apron covered her tight jeans and sweater.

The rest of the gang turned away from their three victims and stared at her. The trio seized their chance and walked off quickly.

'Go on, *Jasper*,' called Vicky. 'Go home with Mummy.'

'It's past your bedtime, *Jasper*,' Lee shouted as Jay's mum crossed the road, and Jay groaned inwardly when he saw the slippers on her feet. She took hold of his arm.

'I've got to get my bike, Mum,' he muttered, pulling away.

'Yeah, don't forget your bike, Jay,' called Lee. 'You'd better take it home and clean it.'

'I think you might have got some dust on the handlebars,' Sean jeered.

Jay heard their laughter echoing behind him and his face burned with embarrassment. It was the worst thing that had ever happened to him.

'I thought I told you to stay away from that lot,' his mum said angrily as she hurried him along the pavement.

'They're my friends.'

'Some friends! They're bullies. I saw what was going on. Why didn't you stop them?'

'I—'

'I've had enough, Jay. Honest, I have. You've been late home every night this week – and now this. I've a good mind to take the plug off that Xbox. It'd serve you right.'

'You can't!'

'Oh, I *can*,' Jay's mum retorted. 'And that's exactly what I'll do if I ever see you hanging around with them again.'

They'd reached the house. Before his mum could say any more Jay pushed his bike through the passage at the side and hung it up in the shed. Then he went straight up to his room and slammed the door behind him, his heart thumping. He heard his dad's voice calling to him half-heartedly, but he knew he wouldn't come up. The football was on the TV, and nothing would tear his dad away from that. He switched on the Xbox and started up *Galactic Explorer*. He'd spent most of the summer holiday playing the game and now he was almost on the final level. He forgot all about his mum and dad and Lee and his mates as he punched coordinates into his ship's computer and navigated through a maze of star systems to the far side of the galaxy . . .

'Jay! Come down here.'

His mum's voice hardly registered. He'd done well and had reached the trickiest part of this level. This was where he'd always failed before and he was determined not to mess it up this time. He fought off missiles from the alien ship that was playing hide-and-seek with him behind the moons of a gas giant planet. Huge plumes of fire kept erupting from the surface below him, and he pushed his ship to the limit as he dodged between them. This was it! He was nearly there—

His bedroom door opened. 'Jasper, get downstairs right now. Me and your dad want to talk to you. Switch that thing off.'

Jay's eyes flicked away from the screen just long enough for an alien photon torpedo to catch him by surprise. His ship exploded spectacularly. He groaned. 'I'd nearly done it, Mum. You made me mess it up.'

His mum pulled the plug out of the socket. 'Downstairs, now,' she said grimly, and Jay knew

8

better than to argue with her when she was in this mood. Reluctantly he followed her down to the living room. On the TV the match had reached half time. His dad hurriedly picked up the remote control and switched it off.

'Right,' said Jay's mum. 'It's time you had a proper activity to do when you're not at school. No more hanging around on street corners. No more coming home late.'

'He wasn't that late,' his dad said. 'You worry too much.'

Jay's mum shot her husband an angry glance. 'You didn't see his so-called friends,' she told him.

'Well, maybe he could try football again. You might be better now you're a bit older,' he said to Jay.

'I'm no good at football, Dad,' Jay replied. 'You know I'm not.'

His dad had been keen for him to play. He'd made him join a Sunday league side, and Jay had spent a whole miserable season shivering on the touchline as a substitute while his dad argued with the coach.

'Not football,' said his mum. 'I think I've found the answer. Look here.'

Jay saw that she had the laptop open on the table. 'What?' he said. Then he saw the screen. '*Scouts?* Mum, you can't be serious.'

'It looks great to me,' she commented. 'Look at all the things you can do: rock climbing, kayaking, snow sports. And you'd *definitely* meet people. Look at all these activity badges you can collect. There's even one for computers.'

'It's just sad, Mum. Why would I want to collect badges? And I already know about computers, don't I? Maybe you should join.'

'Well, maybe I will,' she answered. 'It says here that they need parents to help.'

'Mum!'

'Now you listen to me,' his mum went on firmly. 'You don't have to join straight away. They say you can try it out for a few weeks first, so that's what you're going to do.'

Jay's dad was looking over his shoulder at the list of activities on the computer screen. 'Your mum's right – this looks like fun. You give it a go, Jay. And if it doesn't work out, I can always ring that football coach again and see if he'll have you back.'

Jay knew when he was beaten. 'Can I go now?'

He walked upstairs miserably. He could just imagine what Lee, Sean and Vicky would say if they ever found out he was going to Scouts. But they weren't going to be friends with him now anyway. Not after what had happened earlier. His face felt hot just thinking about it. And when he started secondary school they'd all be there, waiting for him. It was better not to think about any of it. He plugged in the games console again and waited for it to start up. At least he could conquer the galaxy. This time he was going to make it all the way to Level Nine.

CHAPTER 2

When Connor Sutcliff went downstairs, his dad was waiting in the hallway, looking at his watch.

'You don't want to be late,' Dr Sutcliff said. 'It's your big night, right? Your first meeting as Patrol Leader.'

Connor's dad was a GP at the busy local health centre, but he was also a helper at the Sixth Matfield Scout Troop, a job he took very seriously.

'It's OK, Dad,' said Connor, trying not to let on how nervous he felt. 'We always get there before everyone else anyway.'

'Of course we do. If I'm going to help, I'm going to do it properly.' Dr Sutcliff grinned. 'We have to *be prepared*, don't we?!'

Connor groaned. 'You won't make jokes like

that in front of my friends, will you?' he said, heading for the door. Connor was tall for his age, and people often said he looked like his dad. It was true that they both had the same fair hair and blue eyes, but he definitely didn't share his dad's terrible sense of humour.

'Wait, there's something I want to give you before we go. Here . . .'

Connor took the small, battered cardboard box that his dad had handed him. He opened it, then looked up. 'But . . . it's your penknife,' he stammered, looking down at the old white Swiss Army knife.

'Right.' His dad smiled. 'I had it when I was in the Scouts. And it was your grandpa's before that. He gave it to me when *I* became a Patrol Leader. So now it's your turn. Go on, what are you waiting for? Put it in your pocket! It's yours. You can bring it to show your friends, but now we'd better get a move on, or we really *will* be late.'

Connor's mum and his big sister, Ellie, appeared in the living-room doorway.

'Are you sure you don't want to come, Ellie?' asked Dr Sutcliff with a grin.

'No thanks, Dad,' said Ellie. Connor looked at his sister curiously. Her blond hair seemed to have acquired a crimson streak since tea time. 'Me and Mum are going to watch a DVD. It'll be nice and peaceful without Connor in the house.'

'I think you should use the time to add some more streaks to your hair – then you'd look like a—'

'Connor!' said his mum. She turned to her daughter. 'Ellie, it's his first night as Patrol Leader. You might wish him luck.'

Ellie pulled a face and disappeared.

'I'm sure you'll do really well, love,' Connor's mum said, giving him a hug. 'Look at that – I reckon you're as tall as I am now.' She stood back, smiling at him, her grey eyes warm. 'Off you go. Your dad's waiting.'

As he got into the car, Connor's nerves returned. It was almost as bad as when he'd first started secondary school. He didn't feel ready to be a Patrol Leader yet. He was only thirteen – well, thirteen and a half. Mike and Danny, the previous Patrol Leader and Assistant Patrol Leader, were both fourteen so they'd moved up to Explorer Scouts this year. Connor was sure it had been his dad's idea to make him Patrol Leader. He'd accidentally overheard him talking about it to Rick, the Scout Leader of the 6th Matfield Troop, the day before Rick had announced his decision.

When he'd first started at Beavers, Connor hadn't minded his dad being around. It had been fun. But now it seemed like his dad wanted him to do all the things *he'd* done when he was a Scout, only ten times as well. And Connor wasn't sure that was possible.

When they arrived at Scout HQ, Julie, the Assistant Leader, was pinning photos to the notice board near the entrance. 'Hi, Connor, take a look at these. There's some good ones of you and your mates on the crag.' She turned to

Connor's dad. 'Come on, Chris. Rick wants a word. They'll be here soon and we've got a few new kids starting tonight.'

'You didn't get that sun tan in Wales with us,' laughed Connor's dad as the two of them went inside.

'No,' agreed Julie. 'I've been climbing in Arizona.' She was small and wiry, a natural rock climber.

Connor looked at the photos. The summer camp in Wales had been brilliant, and the day they'd spent climbing had been the best of all. He'd been on indoor climbing walls before, but in Wales they'd climbed on rocks high above the valley, with glimpses of the distant sea. It had been amazing. There he was in the photo, reaching up with one hand for an impossibly tiny hold. He remembered the jolt of fear he'd felt when he thought he was about to fall, and the reassuring voice of Mike, the Tigers' previous Patrol Leader, who'd been standing at the foot of the crag feeding out the rope. Then the rush of elation as his fingertips gripped the rock securely and his foot found a solid ledge. There was another picture of him standing at the top, punching the air. He wanted to get his Outdoor Challenge badge this year, and at least one more. He smiled to himself, fingering the knife in his pocket. It would be cool to have more badges than his dad.

'Hi, Connor,' said a quiet voice behind him. 'Are they pictures of the camp?'

Connor turned and saw Toby. The small dark-haired boy was the new Assistant Patrol Leader of the Tigers and, just as importantly, he was Connor's friend. Connor hadn't seen him since the camping trip.

'Yeah, look,' Connor replied. 'There's Tiger Patrol on top of Pen-y-Fan. Thanks to your navigation!'

Toby grinned. 'Mike would have got us there in the end,' he said. 'It's quite easy to go wrong in the mist.'

'Yes, but you were the one who noticed.'

Connor was very glad that Toby was going to be his assistant. Some people thought he was a bit weird, but Connor knew better. Toby's brains had got Tiger Patrol out of trouble on more than one occasion. 'What did you do for the rest of the holidays?' he asked.

'I've been working. I've been helping my mum with her accounts.' Toby's mum had a shop in town, selling dress material.

Connor stared at him. 'What, you've spent your summer holiday doing maths? Now I *know* you're crazy!'

'I'm not, you know,' Toby said, his green eyes glinting. 'I like maths. And besides, Mum paid me. I saved up and bought this.' He rolled up his sleeve. 'It's an altimeter watch,' he explained as more people began to arrive. 'And not just that, it's a compass too, and a barometer. It could measure the height all the way up to the summit of Everest!'

'Well, I don't suppose we'll be going there with Tiger Patrol,' laughed Connor, admiring the watch. 'Look, there are some new Scouts here. Who do you think will be in the Tigers?'

They gazed around the room with interest. They knew most of the faces, but there were four newcomers, including a stocky, pale boy in an oversized sweatshirt with a sulky expression, and a small dark girl with straight black hair and large brown eyes, who was standing a little apart from everyone else. The girl saw them looking, and turned away as the voice of Rick, the Scout Leader, cut through the excited chatter:

'OK, now, everyone, settle down. We need to get started—'

Rick broke off as the door opened and the remaining two members of Tiger Patrol, Andy and Abby, burst into the hall. 'Sorry, Rick,' they said together.

'Andy's dad couldn't find the car keys,' said Abby with a quick wave at Connor and Toby. Her long brown hair was tied back in a ponytail, but several strands had escaped, falling across her face. Connor smiled to himself. Abby could never stay tidy for long.

'What's that?' asked Andy, who was in Connor's class at school. 'Hi, everyone.'

Andy's hair was long too, in the style of a guitarist he admired. He looked quiet and serious most of the time, but there was always a spark of laughter in his brown eyes. Abby nudged him and pointed, and he pulled the headphones out of his ears. 'Sorry' – he grinned – 'I forgot.'

Andy never went anywhere without his iPod. Connor had known him and Abby since Beavers. They lived next door to each other, and they'd been friends pretty much ever since they'd been born.

Like Connor and Toby, they'd been in the Tiger Patrol since they'd all come up from Cubs together two years before. After Flag-break the Scouts stood in a semicircle as Rick spoke to them. The Scout Leader of 6th Matfield was older than Connor's dad, with short, greying hair, but Connor knew he was very fit. He'd run the London marathon earlier that year in a time that Connor, who was in the school cross-country team, knew was very good indeed.

'OK, it's great to have you all back again, and it's good to see so many new faces. We've got an exciting term planned, but before I tell you about it, let's welcome the newcomers. First up is Guy.'

Guy was a tall, gangly black boy with glasses. He stepped forward and waved awkwardly as everyone applauded. Then it was the turn of a girl called Amy to be introduced. She too waved shyly.

'Now,' said Rick, 'Priya. Where are you, Priya?'

'Here.' The small dark girl shook hands with Rick and Julie, then turned to the other Scouts and smiled. 'I'm Priya – my brother is in the Explorer Scouts now, and he had such a lot of fun in the Scouts that I made my dad let me join!' She waved and flashed a brilliant smile, then walked back to her place.

'That was impressive,' whispered Toby. 'I hope she's in the Tigers.'

Connor laughed and nodded. 'Me too.'

'And last but not least,' said Rick, 'we have Jay. Come on, Jay.'

The pale boy in the big sweatshirt shuffled reluctantly to the front. He didn't smile – or even look up when Rick introduced him; then he walked straight back to his place and stood there staring at the floor. Connor caught Andy's eye. Andy raised his eyebrows and shook his head. 'He won't stay long,' Connor whispered to Toby. 'I bet his parents made him come.'

'Well, I didn't like the Scouts much at first, either,' Toby pointed out. 'So you can't tell, not really.'

Connor looked at his friend. Sometimes Toby seemed much older than he really was.

'Right,' said Rick. 'Get together in your Patrols and I'll send you your new members. Guy and Amy, you'll be in Wolf Patrol. Priya and Jay, you're with the Tigers.'

'Hi,' said Priya, walking over to join them. 'Who's the leader?'

'Er, me,' said Connor awkwardly. 'I'm Connor, and Toby's the Assistant Patrol Leader.'

'I know,' replied Priya. 'Didn't you hear me say my brother was in the Scouts? My dad didn't think girls should be Scouts, though. But I went on and on at him and he gave in eventually. He always does.' She paused and smiled at them all. 'What are we doing this term? I hope it's something amazing like windsurfing or rock climbing. How about you, Jay?' She turned to Jay, but he shrugged and looked away.

'These two are Andy and Abby,' Connor told her.

'You're the ones who were late,' said Priya.

'We're always late,' replied Andy, laughing. 'But it's not our fault.'

'Are you twins?' asked Priya.

'No,' said Abby. 'People always think that. Andy's not even my brother. We live next door to each other, that's all.'

'But you do look a bit the same,' Toby said,

glancing at their suntanned faces, freckles and brown hair.

'I know,' said Andy. 'And we have a laugh at school. Some of the teachers *still* think we're twins and we've been there a year now.'

Julie called them all together. 'We're going to play a game,' she announced. 'We've all been standing around talking for long enough. And the game will give you a big clue about our main activity this term. It's called Card Dash. Let's get started.'

The Tigers moved to the end of the hall. Jay sighed loudly before following the others. 'Not much chance of winning the game with him on our team,' Andy muttered in Connor's ear.

'We'll all have to work hard to make up for him,' Connor replied, although privately he agreed with Andy. He could see that being Leader of Tiger Patrol was going to be even harder than he'd thought.

'OK,' said Julie. 'Listen carefully. This is a relay game, so you all line up at the far end of the hall.

Chris has laid out a whole lot of cards at the other end. They all have either a map symbol or a description on them. Your job is to match the symbols with the descriptions. The winning team is the first to get ten matching pairs – and here's the prize.' She held up a large bag of mini chocolate bars.

'We're bound to win now,' Connor said to Andy. 'Abby'll do anything for chocolate.'

Abby gave him a friendly punch. 'I suppose you're not going to eat any when I win them for you?' she said.

But before Connor could reply he heard his dad's voice.

'Good call, Julie!' said Dr Sutcliff. 'Listen, I'll give the Panthers a hand. They've got one Scout missing. That prize is ours, Panthers!'

Connor sighed to himself. Andy shook his head and grinned. 'Don't worry,' he said to Connor. 'Your dad'll probably slow them down. I know *my* dad would!'

'It's great that he wants to join in,' said Priya.

'I think your dad looks sweet!'

Connor couldn't help smiling. Priya seemed to be enthusiastic about absolutely everything. Unlike Jay. He was just standing there, his shoulders slumped, lost in thought. He looked as if he might not join in at all.

'Ready, everyone?' called Rick. 'Three, two, one – go!'

CHAPTER 3

Jay couldn't believe they were taking the game seriously. He moved to the back of the line and watched as Toby, the small dark-haired boy, raced down the hall, picked up two cards and returned, skidding to a halt.

'Give them here,' Priya told Toby as Abby rushed to the far end. 'We should start arranging them now.'

'Good thinking.' Toby smiled, laying his cards on the floor. There was a solid black circle with a cross on the top, and what looked like a stream with a couple of thin black lines across it, and the letters FB beside it. 'Easy,' Toby said, pointing to the black circle. 'That one's a church and the other one's a footbridge.'

Jay thought that Toby might be OK. He

seemed serious but down-to-earth. Connor obviously thought he was really something, being Patrol Leader, but Toby and Priya were doing most of the work. Priya was funny, even if she was a bit bossy. Her jeans and her top looked like they'd come from one of the fashion mags his mum liked reading. The other girl, Abby, was back now, acting like this game was a matter of life and death. She laid her cards down as Connor sprinted away, and Jay felt Andy pushing him forward. He thought Andy's haircut looked stupid, like he was trying to be some kind of rock star.

'You're next,' Andy said encouragingly. 'It's easy.'

'I never said it was hard, did I?' retorted Jay, trying to get out of the way.

But it was too late. Connor was back, slapping him on the arm. 'Go on, Jay,' he said. 'We need to catch up. We're last but one.'

For a moment Jay thought about refusing. Then he shrugged and set off. There was no point getting into a fight, after all. He brought back two cards and put them with the others.

'At last!' said Toby. 'You've got some descriptions. I thought we were going to have nothing but pictures.'

Andy ran next, and then Priya last of all. Tiger Patrol ended up with nine symbols and three descriptions.

'*Church or Chapel with Tower*,' said Toby. 'We've got that one at least.'

'I'm not so sure,' Abby replied doubtfully. 'It doesn't look right to me.'

Jay was interested in spite of himself, mainly because he knew something they didn't. He couldn't resist telling them. He could see that Connor thought he was stupid and it would be fun to surprise him. 'You've got *Electricity Transmission Line* anyway,' he said, pointing to the black line with little V shapes clinging to its side.

Connor looked around the group. They all nodded in agreement. 'Great,' he said. 'Brilliant, Jay. Thanks!'

Jay stared at him. He really *was* stuck up. And annoying too. He was the kind of boy Jay hated. Tall and good-looking, and brilliant at everything. *I bet he's captain of the school football team*, he thought.

'Stop!' called Rick. 'Any cards you haven't paired up go back to the other end, face down. If you haven't decided yet, you still have to put them back. Then we run the relay again.'

Jay had an idea. This wasn't just a race game, and he'd thought of a way to gain an edge over the other teams. 'I'll put them back,' he said to Toby, and took the pile of cards from him, ignoring the surprised looks from the others. When he reached the end of the hall he positioned the cards carefully, checking the pictures and writing as he placed them face down.

'Get a move on,' said Connor as Jay walked back. 'They're all ready.'

Jay ignored him. Connor thought he was so clever, but he didn't have a clue how to win this game.

Rick blew his whistle and Toby flew down the hall. Priya knelt on the floor, arranging the cards neatly as each patrol member returned. When the round was finished, Jay stood to one side and watched them matching up the cards. They made two more pairs, but there were several pictures left over.

'That one's a cliff,' said Toby.

'Right,' agreed Connor. 'And that's a bridleway. But they're no use without the descriptions.'

'Here,' said Jay. 'I'll put them back.'

He heard Andy mutter, 'What's he looking so pleased about?' but he ignored him and went down the hall to put the cards carefully in position. As he returned he could see that Connor was getting angry and trying not to let it show. He obviously had a bit of a temper, and was used to getting his own way. Jay deliberately slowed down and tried not to laugh as Connor's face turned even redder.

The whistle blew for the next round of relays,

and Toby was off. When Jay saw the pictures he'd brought back, he grinned to himself. Abby set off, and then Connor, and they made two more pairs.

'Go on, Jay,' yelled Connor. 'Run! They're going to beat us!'

Ahead of him Jay heard Connor's dad shout, 'Yes!' and hold up a card, just like he was a big kid. The Panthers must be nearly there. The rest of their team were all jumping up and down in excitement.

'Nice one, Chris!' called Sajiv, the Panthers' Patrol Leader. 'We only need one more!'

Jay strolled to the other end. This was fun. He picked up the two cards he needed. He knew exactly where they were. Then, as the last of the Panthers agonized over which card to choose, he walked quickly back to the other Tigers and matched up the cards. 'There!' he said.

He saw Connor's mouth fall open. 'How did you—?'

'Connor!' said Abby. 'We've won! Sit down, quick!'

Rick saw them sitting on the floor and blew his whistle. There were loud groans from the other teams, and the Panthers couldn't believe their eyes. 'That can't be right,' said Connor's dad.

Jay glanced at him. He was like a grown-up version of Connor. He wondered what Connor thought about his dad acting like a kid. He remembered his own dad jumping up and down on the touchline at football matches. It had been embarrassing.

The Tigers waited nervously as Rick checked their pairs. 'All correct,' he announced, smiling. 'Nice work, Tigers. I thought the Panthers had it won. Great teamwork, all of you.'

'That was really cool,' said Abby.

'Yeah,' Andy agreed. 'They thought they'd beaten us.'

'But how did you do it?' Toby asked.

'Well,' began Jay, 'I—'

'You didn't cheat, did you?' Connor said suddenly, his face darkening. 'Because if you did . . .'

Toby touched Connor's arm. 'Of course he didn't cheat,' he said, fixing his green eyes on Jay. 'Go on, Jay, tell us.'

Jay shook his head. It was obvious that Connor had it in for him. He wasn't going to tell him anything, not now.

'I bet I know what you did,' said Priya, smiling. 'You memorized the cards, didn't you, when you put them back? Very clever!'

'Cool,' said Toby, when Jay couldn't help smiling back at Priya. 'We should have thought of that.'

'Is that right?' Connor asked awkwardly.

Jay shrugged. He was still smarting over Connor's accusation.

'I'm sorry,' Connor said. 'I should have realized . . .'

Jay turned away, ignoring him.

'Hey, everyone,' said Rick, waving his hands to get the Scouts' attention. 'That was really good. Congratulations to Tiger Patrol!'

The team cheered loudly as Rick threw the

34

bag of chocolates. Connor caught it deftly, and opened it up for them all to share.

Rick continued, 'Now, this term we're all going to try for our Orienteering Badge. I'm glad you're all getting on so well with those Ordnance Survey symbols, because you're going to have to learn a whole lot of new ones for orienteering!'

'That's not fair,' said Sajiv. 'Why can't we use the normal ones?'

'We'll be using special maps,' explained Rick. 'They're much more detailed. At an orienteering event you have to navigate between checkpoints using a map and a compass . . .'

Jay stopped listening, focusing instead on the taste of the chocolate melting in his mouth. There wasn't any point in listening because by the time they started doing whatever stupid activities Rick had planned, *he* wasn't going to be here. He looked at Connor, who was listening to Rick like it was the most important thing he'd ever heard. Idiot.

'Is it like a race?' Andy asked Rick, his voice cutting into Jay's thoughts.

'Kind of,' Rick answered. 'It's a race where you don't know where you'll be going before the start. We'll be having our first practice in the park in a couple of weeks. After that there's a proper orienteering event at Nash Hall Country Park, where even complete beginners can join in. Then, before half term, we'll take part in a big event on the moors. If you complete that course, you should all get your badges. I've done a printout of the orienteering map symbols for you to take home.'

'I thought you did well,' said Connor's dad as they got into the car after the meeting. They were the last to leave – as usual. 'I was impressed that you won the game. What did you make of the new recruits?'

Connor looked where his dad was pointing. Jay was walking down the road, and Toby was talking to him.

'Toby's trying really hard,' said Connor. 'But I don't think it'll do any good. Anyone can see Jay won't stay long.'

'You can never tell,' his dad replied. 'If you're going to be a good Patrol Leader, you'll have to learn to get on with all sorts, won't you?'

Connor glanced at him. Jay had been really annoying, and he couldn't see how he'd *ever* get on with him. He wondered if his dad had noticed them arguing. But Dr Sutcliff had moved on to another subject now. 'You'd better get stuck into learning those orienteering symbols when we get home,' he said. 'I'll test you on them tomorrow.'

Connor tried not to sigh out loud. Ever since Rick had decided to make him Patrol Leader, his dad had been on his case the whole time. It wasn't enough just to be Patrol Leader – Connor had to be the best Patrol Leader ever. That was what it seemed like anyway. He glanced back out of the window as they drove off. Toby was still talking to Jay.

*

Jay didn't want Toby tagging along with him. He was still wearing his Scout uniform, and the last thing he needed was for Lee, Sean or Vicky to see them together.

'How come you knew about the electricity symbol?' Toby asked. 'I'd totally forgotten it.'

Jay shrugged and kept on walking, hoping he would give up and go away.

'You must have enjoyed yourself a bit,' Toby persisted. 'I mean, it was pretty cool how you worked out the game. You must have a good memory too. Plus, I thought I saw you smile once.'

'I thought it was the stupidest thing I've ever seen,' said Jay, stopping suddenly. 'Why would anyone want to collect badges? It's like getting stickers at school. It's pointless. And that boy, Connor – he's a pain in the neck.'

'You've got him all wrong,' Toby said hotly. 'Connor's all right. If you knew him properly you'd never say that.' He paused. 'Anyway,' he went on more calmly, 'we do good things in the Scouts. Things you can't do normally – like rock climbing and kayaking and—'

'And finding your way around a country park?' said Jay scornfully. 'In the rain, most probably, with a map and a compass. I've been there with my mum and dad. They have paths signposted everywhere. And I know my way home, thanks. I don't need you following me.'

Jay strode off quickly. He felt bad for a moment because he knew that Toby was only trying to be friendly, but he shouldn't have kept going on at him. Scouts had been terrible – exactly how he'd thought it would be. OK, he'd enjoyed the game a bit, and most of the other kids had been all right – apart from Connor. But there was no way he was going trudging around the countryside in the rain and mud. He just had to get through the next few weeks, hope that Lee and the gang didn't see him with the Scouts, and then maybe his mum would let him stop.

He couldn't wait to leave.

CHAPTER 4

It was a Saturday morning two weeks later, and for once Connor was in more of a hurry than his dad. 'I'm going round to get Andy and Abby,' he said, spreading a thick layer of peanut butter on three pieces of buttered toast. 'I want to make sure all the Tigers arrive on time today. I'm going to get a lift with them.'

Rick had moved this week's meeting to a Saturday so that they could have their first go at orienteering, and Connor knew that his dad had already driven to the park with Rick to get things ready before returning to have breakfast. Connor poured himself a large glass of milk and sat down at the dining table to eat his breakfast.

'Just make sure those two don't make *you* late as well,' his dad replied. 'I've got to stop in at the surgery on the way, so I'll see you there.' He turned away to answer the phone.

Just as Connor was finishing his toast, his dad called out to him, 'Here – Grandpa's on the phone. He wants a word before you go.'

Connor gulped down the last of his milk and took the handset from his dad.

'All right, Connor?' his grandpa asked him. 'You've got the knife, then?'

'Yes,' replied Connor. 'It's brilliant.'

'It's useful too. That knife has got me out of some tricky situations. Did I ever tell you about that time in the Alps when—'

'I'm sorry, Grandpa,' Connor cut in. 'I can't talk now. We're going orienteering this morning.' He knew if he let his grandpa get started on one of his stories, he'd never get away.

'No worries,' replied his grandpa. 'Enjoy yourself, Connor. And don't get lost!'

Connor shook his head as he put the phone down, but he couldn't help smiling. His grandpa's jokes were even worse than his dad's. 'I'm off now, Dad,' he called. 'I'll see you at HQ.'

He jogged all the way to Andy's house, where he found him and Abby standing in the driveway beside the car. 'What's up?' he said. 'Why are you waiting?'

'It's Dad,' said Andy. 'Mum asked him to put the washing on before we left and he forgot. He's just coming.'

'Where's the detergent, Andy?' came Mr Mackenzie's voice from inside the house. 'I can't find it anywhere.'

'I'd better go and help,' Andy said with an air of resignation.

'Don't worry,' Abby told Connor. 'We've got plenty of time.'

'We really should get going,' replied Connor, looking at his watch. He didn't want to hassle too much but he knew that Rick would notice if they showed up late.

Just then Mr Mackenzie appeared in the doorway in jeans and a crumpled T-shirt. 'Hi, Connor,' he said as Andy slammed the front door. 'It looks like we'll be on time for once. Into the car, everyone.'

'Oh, no!' Andy clutched his head. 'I forgot my camcorder!'

He unlocked the front door while the others got into the car. Connor looked at his watch again, but Abby laughed as Andy came rushing back outside and flung himself into the back seat. 'You're just as bad as your dad,' she said.

'No I'm not,' retorted Andy. 'That's the first time I—'

'Hey,' said Abby, turning round from the front passenger seat to poke him. 'I was only teasing.'

'So what are you actually doing at Scouts this term?' Mr Mackenzie asked over his shoulder. 'You told me once, but I've forgotten.'

'Orienteering's the main thing,' Connor replied.

'That's what we're doing today,' said Andy. 'That's why I need my camcorder.'

'You won't win any orienteering events if you spend all your time filming,' Mr Mackenzie said.

'The others will be miles ahead of you. It's all about racing through the countryside, isn't it? You don't want anything to slow you down.'

'Well, *I* think it'll be useful,' said Andy stubbornly.

Connor caught Mr Mackenzie winking at Abby. He'd known all along that Andy's dad was only joking: he could be very funny indeed – especially when he was telling Andy's friends about the crazy things that happened to him in his job as a news cameraman with the local TV station – but he'd always taken Andy's film-making seriously and he was very proud of his son's achievements. Connor had known Andy for a long time and he'd always loved everything to do with cameras and filming. All the best photos of the summer camp were Andy's.

'If I make a really good film,' Andy continued, 'then it could be helpful to people who haven't gone orienteering before. It might even be useful to us. Like, it might show the mistakes we make.'

'I'm not going to make any,' said Abby with a grin.

'I bet you will,' replied Andy. 'You'll go zooming off at a hundred miles an hour and then you'll find the only patch of mud and fall over in it.'

'No I won't – just because I accidentally slipped in that ditch at camp—'

'And you fell in the river when we were fishing, and you turned your face black with smoke when you were trying to get the fire going, and—'

Abby gave him a withering look. 'I'm good at lots of things,' she said. 'You know I am.'

'It's true,' said Connor, smiling. Hanging out with Andy and Abby was like being in a whirlwind at times, he thought, but they were a lot of fun.

Andy laughed, then switched on the camcorder and pointed it at Abby's face. She stuck out her tongue and turned to Mr Mackenzie. 'I think Andy's right – it'll be great to have a record of everything we do this term.'

'Yes,' agreed Connor. 'And when the Tigers do really well, we'll have a movie to prove it.'

'Right,' said Andy as they pulled into the car park. 'But just remember we've got Jay in Tiger Patrol. I don't think he's too keen. Look!'

Outside the entrance to Scout HQ, Jay was arguing with his mum. Whatever he was saying, his mum didn't want to listen. She got into her car and drove off quickly, leaving Jay standing there. He saw Andy and Abby and Connor watching, and flushed before turning to go inside.

'Hmmm,' said Mr Mackenzie, raising his eyebrows slightly. 'I see what you mean.'

'Let's get moving,' said Rick, once everyone had arrived. 'We're going to walk to the park. Chris, Julie and I have laid out an orienteering course for you, and we've got lots of helpers. We'll give you your maps and other instructions when we get there. Let's go.'

When they reached the park, Rick asked each patrol to split up into pairs.

'Can you go with Jay?' Connor asked Toby. 'I'll go with Priya. They're both new so they're bound to need help.'

'I have actually used a map and a compass before,' Priya told him brightly, a spark of mischief in her dark eyes.

'Oh,' said Connor, embarrassed. 'Right. Well, great. I bet we'll do really well. Andy, you go with Abby.'

'Listen, everyone,' said Rick. 'The helpers will bring you a master map. Copy down the locations of the control points onto your own maps. Do it accurately, the way we've practised. When you're ready, come to the start and I'll send you off. Your rounds will be timed from there. Whoever gets round the course in the fastest time wins. You'll need to get your card stamped by the helper at each control point. Understood?'

They all nodded.

'OK,' Rick continued. 'Now, it'll be up to you

to decide which route you take to reach each control point. In some cases it might actually be faster to go across the park or through the trees using a compass. But if you don't use the map and the compass properly, it may well take you longer.'

Connor's dad was helping Tiger Patrol. He leaned the large master map against a tree, then handed a smaller map and a red pen to each pair. 'Get copying,' he said. 'I'll see you out on the course. I'm going to have a run around it myself, just to keep my hand in. Good luck, Tigers. And Connor, remember what Grandpa said!'

'What did he mean?' Priya asked as Connor's dad walked away.

'It was a joke,' said Connor, smiling to himself. Then he looked up and saw that Andy had his camcorder in his hand and his iPod headphones in his ears. 'Andy!' he exclaimed. 'We're going to need your help, you know.'

'I tried to tell him,' said Abby as Andy pointed

the camcorder at two boys from Kestrel Patrol, who were arguing over their map.

Andy reluctantly switched off the camcorder and took out the headphones, still nodding his head in time to the music he'd been listening to. 'I think I've got some decent footage, but I do need to film as much as possible, you know.'

'You might want to start on your map,' Connor pointed out.

'Don't worry,' Andy replied confidently, fitting the camcorder into its case. 'We're both faster runners than you are. We're the fastest in the troop. I bet we'll catch you up. Right, Abby?'

'You bet,' Abby agreed. 'And anyway, Connor, you haven't done *your* map yet, have you?'

'No,' said Connor, flustered. 'But—'

'It's all right,' said Priya, who was crouching down, her map lying on a patch of clear ground. 'I've finished.'

Connor looked over at her disbelievingly, his gaze moving quickly to the map in her hand.

'It's a good job someone on your team's doing

some work!' laughed Abby, poking him playfully on the arm.

Connor came closer to Priya. 'Are you sure that's right?' he asked her. 'You did it incredibly quickly.'

'Of course I'm sure,' she said, standing up and tossing back her long black hair. She flashed him a confident grin. 'We're ready. Let's go.'

She headed for the start. Connor had a quick look to see how Toby and Jay were getting on – Toby was copying the route and Jay was watching – then hurried after Priya. Up ahead, they reached Julie, who checked their map.

'Well done, you two,' she told them. 'You're the first. Very accurate and quick.'

Priya smiled at Connor.

'Actually, Priya did it all,' Connor said, with a nod towards the Tigers' newest recruit.

'Excellent,' replied Julie, glancing at him. 'Looks like you'll all have to be on your toes to keep up with her. Let's hope you can find your way around just as fast, Priya. Here's your card.

There'll be a helper at each control point by the time you get there. Off you go.'

Priya set off at once, heading down a long, curving path towards a clump of trees. She was wearing running pants and a sweatshirt but she still managed to look cooler than anyone else. Connor hesitated for a second, then sprinted to catch up with her. She slowed to a jog. 'I've worked it out,' she said. 'The first control point is on the far side of those trees.'

'Wait a bit,' said Connor, and Priya stopped. 'We're supposed to have the map the right way round all the time, with our thumb on it to keep track of where we are.'

'You're just like my brother,' Priya told him. 'He's always really, really careful. And a bit boring too,' she added with a cheeky grin.

Connor felt himself go red, but before he could think of a neat retort she continued: 'Are you coming, or not? Look, the others will catch us up.'

Connor glanced back and saw Toby and Jay

setting off. He took the map that Priya was offering him and had a quick look. He was pretty sure she had it right. 'OK,' he said. 'Let's go.'

They jogged off along the track. Connor was starting to feel sorry for Priya's big brother. *It must be hard work living with her all the time. I'm the Patrol Leader, after all*, he told himself. *When we get to the control point, I'm going to make sure we do the next bit* my *way.*

CHAPTER 5

Jay watched Connor follow Priya into the distance. Turning to Toby, he saw he was holding the map. 'What are you doing?' he asked. It was the first time he'd spoken since Connor had asked Toby to work with him.

'You can still talk, then?' said Toby, his finger tracing over a path on the map.

'Yeah, well, I was in a bad mood. I had a row with my mum.'

'Parents can be hard work.' Toby nodded sympathetically. 'I'm just lining the map up with the real world,' he said. 'So we can see what we're doing.'

Jay looked over his shoulder and it immediately made sense to him. 'There are three ways to get to that first point,' he said to Toby.

'And I reckon that one's the shortest.' He pointed to a narrow path that snaked around to the right of the clump of trees. 'Much shorter than the way those two went,' he added, looking at Connor and Priya. He saw the surprise in Toby's green eyes. *He's probably wondering why I'm so interested*, Jay thought to himself. *I don't blame him, after the way I acted last time.*

Toby consulted the map. He pulled a compass out of his pocket and took careful measurements with the scale on the edge. 'You're right,' he said. 'But how did you work it out so fast?'

'Boys!' interrupted Rick, who had been watching them with an amused smile on his face. 'You can discuss it on the way. Off you go! Next pair, get ready.'

Jay and Toby walked quickly down the path. 'No need to run,' said Toby. 'Not with a short-cut expert on the team. Go on, tell me how you did it.'

'*Galactic Explorer*,' Jay replied. 'You know – the game . . . on Xbox . . . I've been prospecting for heavy metals in a planetary system in the Black Eye Galaxy, and you have to choose the shortest path through the methane swamps.'

'But that's on Level Nine!' said Toby. 'I've read about it. I've got that game and I can't get past the Borgons' ship *Phantom* in Arcturus. I've been trying for weeks and I'm still stuck on Level Five.'

Jay laughed. He was surprised to find that Toby was into *Galactic Explorer*, but he wasn't a bit surprised that he was stuck on Level Five. It was very tricky. 'No problem – did you disable the force fields and the invisibility screen? You have to hack into the *Phantom*'s computer using the access code that you get when you land on the third moon of Borgon.'

'Wow!' said Toby as they made their way past the clump of trees. 'I would never have thought of that. Thanks! And look – that's the control point over there, with the orange triangle.'

Jay warmed at Toby's praise. Maybe this day wasn't going to be so bad, after all.

'Look, there's Connor and Priya,' said Jay. 'We've nearly caught them up.'

'Yes!' Toby held up a hand and Jay gave him a high-five, although he couldn't help feeling a little awkward about doing it.

Connor and Priya glanced up the slope when they heard Toby's voice. He laughed at the comical expressions on their faces. 'It's not just about running fast,' he called down to them. 'You have to use your brains too.'

Priya laughed, took a quick look at the map in Connor's hand, and set off across a football pitch.

'Looks like Priya's in charge,' Toby said as they jogged over to the control point, where a helper was waiting to stamp their card. 'Now, tell me what else I have to do to get to Level Six in that game.'

Connor and Priya worked their way steadily around the course. Connor had to admit that Priya was very good at map-reading, so it hadn't really been a problem when she kept running on ahead. If he started to feel annoyed, he told himself that she was a lot younger than him, and she was probably just trying to impress him.

They only had three control points left to find when they met Andy and Abby on the path near the skate park. Andy had stopped to film Abby as she looked at the map; her hair, as usual, had escaped from its ponytail and was blowing in her face.

'How are you getting on?' asked Connor. 'We've nearly finished.'

'We're on our way to control point five,' Abby replied, showing Connor her map. 'I bet we're actually catching you up.'

'I doubt it,' said Connor, trying to look confident. He wasn't going to let on, but secretly he was worried that Abby was right. She and Andy had obviously been going very fast.

'Are you going to film us too?' asked Priya.

'Sure,' said Andy. 'If you like.'

'No way!' said Connor. 'You're just trying to slow us down.'

'Don't be daft,' said Andy. 'It slows us down too.'

'Yes,' said Connor, 'and then Toby and Jay will beat all of us.'

'*I'll* do it,' laughed Abby. 'And while I'm filming, you can work out where we're meant to go next, Andy. You haven't done any map-reading yet. You'll never learn anything if you don't.'

'OK, then,' said Andy. 'Put the strap over your hand and hold it steady. And don't mess about with the zoom while you're shooting. I prefer separate shots. Maybe a mid-shot and then a close-up.'

'Are you trying to annoy me?' asked Abby. 'You've told me all that stuff a million times. Go on, you two,' she said to Connor and Priya. 'Pretend to look at the map and I'll film you going off into the distance.'

'Action!' called Andy, pretending to snap a clapperboard with his hands.

Connor and Priya looked at their map, then

started walking down the path, but they had only gone a few paces when Connor heard the sound of wheels behind them. Three teenagers on bikes raced past, nearly knocking Priya onto the grass. There were two boys and a girl.

'Hey!' Connor yelled, 'Watch what you're doing!'

The kids skidded round the corner into the skate park and began riding up and down the ramps. Andy took the camcorder back from Abby and filmed them for a few seconds.

'What do you want to film *them* for?' demanded Connor, red spots of anger on his cheeks.

'Background,' Andy replied. 'I'm going to get some shots of those dog-walkers too. It'll make the movie more interesting to watch.'

'Does Andy do that all the time?' Priya asked as she and Connor jogged away. 'Filming, I mean?'

'He's brilliant at it,' replied Connor. 'I bet he'll end up at art college one day. He made a movie of our last summer camp and edited it all on his computer. You should see it.'

'I'd like to – I can't believe they're catching us up when they keep stopping like that.'

'You don't know them. They weren't just boasting about being fast runners. They really are. And Abby's clever too. She can probably read a map even better than you.'

'So can Jay and Toby,' Priya said. 'Look – there they come!' She glanced down at the map. 'I've got it!' she said excitedly. 'We can take a short cut. We can run through that group of trees right there. I bet that's what they'll do. We don't want them to catch us, do we?'

She thrust the map at Connor and dashed off up the hill. As soon as he looked at the map, he knew that she'd made a mistake. There was a band of thick undergrowth all around the wood. They'd never be able to get through it and they'd waste valuable time if they tried. 'Hey, Priya!' he called. 'Come back!'

But either Priya was too far away to hear him,

or she simply didn't want to listen. Connor set off in pursuit, but by the time he reached the edge of the trees, she was already ploughing though a tangle of brambles and stinging nettles. 'It's no good, there isn't a way through. It says on the map,' he shouted.

'Ouch!' exclaimed Priya, prising a bramble off her leg. 'Are you sure?'

'It was a good idea,' replied Connor. 'I suppose it isn't really that obvious that you can't get through.'

Priya had made her way back to him and was looking at the map. 'Eek!' she said. 'Sorry, Connor. I guess we'll just have to go round.'

'Yes. But which way?'

'I'm not sure. You decide.'

'Who, me?' Connor pretended to be astonished.

'What? I'm not bossy *all* the time, you know! I even let my brother tell me what to do sometimes.'

'OK,' said Connor with a grin. 'But we'd better run. There are Jay and Toby.'

They looked back and saw the two boys coming up the hill towards them. Connor noticed that Jay was keeping up with Toby easily. He'd assumed that Jay was unfit, with his pale face and sulky look, but under that outsize sweatshirt he obviously wasn't as out of shape as he looked.

'Let's hope they make the same mistake I did,' Priya said as they sprinted away.

They'd chosen the right direction and soon they were following a shaded path around the edge of the wood. 'The control is on a sign or notice board,' Connor said, glancing at the map. 'It should be about two hundred metres north of here. That's straight towards the park entrance.'

They set off across the grass.

'There's a sign,' he said, pointing. It was twenty metres away and it said NO BALL GAMES.

'It's too soon,' Priya replied. 'I've been counting steps. We've only come sixty metres.'

Connor looked at her with new respect. 'Excellent! In that case, it must be that one there, the big one.'

They raced forward and found the control marker hanging under a notice board that advertised events in the park.

'That's it.' Connor stamped their card. 'All we have to do now is get back to the start. I bet no one's been faster than us.'

They turned to run down the path, and immediately found their way blocked by the three teenagers on bikes they'd seen earlier.

'What's that, then?' demanded a girl with spiky black hair, pointing at the control point.

'It's for orienteering,' said Connor, feeling his heart beating faster and wondering what to do. This lot seemed to be looking for trouble and he didn't want to make things worse. 'It's a sport. You have to find your way around using a map.'

'Why would you want to do that?' said the taller of the two boys. 'What's the point?'

Connor took a deep breath. 'Because it's fun?'

he offered. 'And it helps you to learn to use a compass.'

'We have to go,' Priya's voice trembled slightly. 'We're in a race.'

'Oh, yeah?' said the girl. She kept her bike right in the middle of the path, blocking their way.

'Excuse me,' Connor interrupted politely. 'Come on, Priya.' He stepped forward, looking the girl straight in the eye. Beneath the politeness there was an edge to his voice.

After a second the girl looked away, and moved her bike back just enough to let the two of them through.

As they walked on down the path, Connor heard one of the boys mimicking him. 'Excuse me,' he said. 'I'm such a polite little Scout.'

'Love the uniform,' yelled the girl, and they all burst out laughing.

'That was good,' said Priya, looking approvingly at Connor. 'It was like something out of a movie.'

'There's the finish,' said Connor – he didn't want to talk about it. His heart was thumping in his chest. The two boys had looked mean, and right up to the last moment he'd thought that one of them might throw a punch. Maybe it would have been better to have turned round and walked away, but they'd made him angry. They'd really scared Priya. 'Come on,' he said. 'Let's run.'

Behind them, Jay and Toby were coming round the corner of the wood.

'We can still beat them,' said Toby. 'They started about four minutes ahead of us. It's a hundred metres to the control and another two hundred to the finish. We can do that in less than four minutes, can't we?'

Jay didn't reply. He felt sick. Lee and Sean and Vicky were there on the grass, right ahead of them. They hadn't seen him yet, but any second they were going to.

'What's up, Jay?' asked Toby, turning back. 'You've gone white.'

'That lot over there,' Jay said. 'I don't want them to see me.'

'Why not?'

'I just don't, OK? They go to my school. There's no way I'm going over there.'

Lee, Sean and Vicky had given Jay a hard time when he'd first started school. Vicky especially had enjoyed doing impressions of Jay's mum in her slippers. Jay had tried to avoid them, but it hadn't been easy. There had been some bad moments. The last thing he needed was for them to see him with the Scouts.

'They're bullies, aren't they?' Toby asked.

Jay shrugged. 'I guess,' he muttered.

'Better keep out of their way, then,' Toby said calmly. 'That's what I always do.'

'You . . . ?' began Jay.

'We'll just have to go the long way round,' Toby continued. 'I never expected to win anyway.' And he set off in the other direction.

Jay watched him for a moment before

following on behind. Toby kept on surprising him. First the computer games, now this. A lot of people would have thought he was just being stupid about Lee and the others, but Toby had understood straight away. He was actually sort of all right.

Back at Scout HQ Rick told them their times. 'Tiger Patrol, it was very close between Connor and Priya, and Jay and Toby. Well done, you four. But the winners by five seconds were Abby and Andy.'

'I don't believe it!' exclaimed Connor. 'You kept stopping all the time.'

'We did warn you,' said Abby. 'You and Priya went wrong at the wood, and Jay and Toby lost some time as well. We just kept going. Plus we're better than you!'

There was no time for the others to argue about it because at that moment Connor's dad came through the door. 'Biscuits and juice, anyone?' he asked, bending down to place a large container, a thermos and plastic cups on a table near the door.

A cheer went up from the Scouts, and Connor gave his dad a warm smile.

Rick waited patiently until everyone had taken their fill of snacks, before making his final announcement. 'Thanks to Dr Sutcliff for the refreshments. Next week we'll have a session on first aid.'

'I'll pay special attention next week, then,' said Andy, brushing crumbs off his shirt. ''Cos sooner or later I'm bound to have to give first aid to Abby. She's always bombing on ahead without looking.'

'I am not,' retorted Abby. 'It's you who's going to have an accident. You'll probably fall over a cliff and break your leg while you're looking through that viewfinder.'

Connor watched them go out to the car, laughing. Jay and Toby said goodbye and walked off down the street together. 'Bye, Connor,' said Priya, with a little wave. 'Shame we didn't win. I thought we were a good team.'

Connor grinned, embarrassed but pleased. 'Right,' he said gruffly. 'See you next week.'

Priya ran to meet her dad, who was standing beside his car. A tall boy got out of the passenger seat – Connor guessed it was Priya's big brother. He messed up her hair as she reached him, and she punched him on the arm. As she got into the car, she turned and gave Connor a final wave. That was the best thing about Scouts, he thought as his dad came out with Rick. You were always making new friends, and often your new friends were the most unexpected people. Even Jay looked like he'd enjoyed the orienteering. Maybe Tiger Patrol was going to turn out well after all.

CHAPTER 6

The following Thursday after school there was a knock on the Watsons' front door. Jay ran down the stairs two at a time. 'It's for me, Mum,' he yelled. 'Toby told me he'd call round tonight.'

'Toby? Who's Toby.'

'He's from Scouts. He's come round so I can show him how to get to the next level on *Galactic*.'

Jay opened the door to see Toby waiting on the doorstep with an enormous rucksack over his shoulder.

'Well now,' said Mrs Watson, wiping her hands on her apron as she came out of the kitchen. 'I'm very glad Jay's making friends at Scouts, but I didn't think Scouts would be interested in computer games. Jay wastes enough time on them already. He's got a lovely mountain bike out the back that he looks after like it was a baby, but he hardly ever rides it these days.'

Jay prayed his mum would stop talking. If she kept this up, Toby would never come round again.

'Scouts do lots of things,' Toby said earnestly. 'Even biking. But Jay's a real expert at *Galactic Explorer*. There aren't many people in the whole country who've got as far as he has. He's going to give me some help.'

Jay looked at him gratefully. For once his mum was at a loss for words, and he seized the chance to take Toby up to his room.

'Right,' he said, shutting his bedroom door. 'I've got it all set up. I'll show you how to get the access codes for the ship. Here, you take the controller.'

'That's brilliant,' said Toby twenty minutes later. 'Don't show me any more. I reckon I can make it to Level Six on my own now.'

Jay moved away as Toby took over the controls once again. 'I think the guy who invented that game might have been a bit mad,' he said, bending over a huge cardboard box filled with more games. 'I've got something else here you might want to try . . .'

He heard the door open and looked up to see his mum standing there with a tray piled high with muffins. 'I expect you're hungry,' she said to Toby. 'I made these yesterday but I've warmed them up for you in the microwave. If I'd known you were coming I'd have baked fresh,' she finished, with an accusing look at Jay. 'They're cheese and ham – Jay's favourite.'

Jay's ears went pink and he looked over at Toby, waiting for his reaction.

'Amazing, thanks very much! They smell delicious, Mrs Watson.' Toby helped himself to a large muffin and happily took the napkin that Jay's mother offered him. Jay took a muffin as well, muttering thanks to his mum.

After they had finished eating, Jay continued

his search through his collection and Toby took the controls again.

'Don't you think orienteering is a bit like a computer game?' Toby asked. 'The way you have to search places and collect things, and race against the clock?'

'I guess,' agreed Jay. He looked up at Toby. 'You're trying to get me to join the Scouts properly, aren't you?'

'Well, why not?' Toby glanced over for a second before turning back to the screen. 'You're really good with maps. We need you in Tiger Patrol. Next week we're going to Nash Hall Country Park, and by the time we do the last challenge on the moors we'll need to be experts at navigation. We do cycling too,' he added. 'Is that right about the mountain bike?'

'Dad used to take me out to ride trails,' Jay said. 'Then he got too unfit to keep up with me so we stopped going. He made me try football instead, but I hated that.'

'Shame,' said Toby. 'But maybe you can

come biking with us. There's a badge, you know.'

'I'm not sure,' Jay said, sitting down beside him, clutching a DVD case.

'You're not still worried about those kids we saw in the park . . . They won't know you're going to Scouts, will they? And anyway, you can't let them spoil your life.'

'I don't want to talk about it,' said Jay. 'Finish up what you're doing and I'll show you this new game I got last week.'

'He seemed like a nice boy,' Jay's mum said after Toby had left.

'Yeah,' said Jay. 'He's all right.'

'So, shall we go and get your uniform then? Next week, before this big outing of yours?'

Jay hesitated. He'd been thinking about what Toby had said. The orienteering in the park had been brilliant until Lee and his mates appeared – just as interesting as most computer games. And he could always wear a hoodie over the uniform when he was walking home. 'Yeah,' he told his mum. 'OK, then.'

'That's great,' she said, and she gave him a big wet kiss which almost made him change his mind.

It was breakfast time on the day of the trip to Nash Hall Country Park, and while Connor tried to eat his cereal, his dad was giving him a lecture about how to succeed at orienteering.

'This event is mainly in woodland,' Dr Sutcliff said. 'I hope Rick's going to get you to try an orange course at least. You really should be starting to do some proper navigation. It's a pity he doesn't take you up on the moors to practise. They're much nearer than this country park.'

'It's only our second attempt, Dad,' Connor replied. 'Some people had never even held a compass before that time in the park.'

'Well, even so,' said his dad. 'If Rick gives you a choice of courses to do, you make sure that Tiger Patrol takes on something challenging.'

'Leave the poor boy alone, Chris,' said Connor's mum. 'Maybe you should stay here and fix those fence panels in the garden. That would be a lot more useful than chasing around in the woods. You're not fourteen any more, you know.'

'I can still run as fast as most of those kids,' Dr Sutcliff replied. 'Can't I, Connor?'

'Sure, Dad,' said Connor with a sigh. He wished his dad wouldn't insist on joining in with races and games at every opportunity. It was seriously embarrassing.

'Well, have a great day, both of you,' said his mum. 'I'm going shopping in town with Ellie. Sure you wouldn't rather come with us?'

Connor and his dad both laughed. Connor went to fetch the rucksack he'd packed carefully the night before, and they drove off towards Scout HQ.

'Isn't that Jay?' asked Connor's dad as they passed a boy walking slowly along the street in an outsize hoodie.

'Yes,' said Connor, looking back. 'I thought

Toby said he was going to buy his uniform. Looks like he was wrong. Hey! Look out, Dad!'

Dr Sutcliff braked sharply as two boys and a girl on bikes skidded across the road in front of them and rode off along the pavement, laughing.

'I've seen them before,' Connor said. 'They were in the park when we were orienteering.'

'They'll get themselves killed,' his dad muttered. 'That could have been nasty.'

Connor looked back and saw the gang ride past Jay, who flattened himself against the fence to let them through. Jay waited until they'd gone, then carried on along the pavement.

At Scout HQ two minibuses were waiting. Andy and Abby were already there, and Andy filmed Connor getting out of his car.

'How did you manage it?' Connor asked him. 'Did you find the keys yourself?'

'Easier than that.' Andy grinned. 'Abby's mum brought us. Hey, look! Here comes Priya in her uniform. I have to get this.'

He pointed the camcorder down the street as

Priya waved goodbye to her dad and started walking towards them. 'This is great footage,' he said as Jay came round the corner and saw Priya. 'Hey, Connor, look – Jay's wearing his uniform under that hoodie! Jay – take off your hoodie. For the camera!'

Jay looked over and then, a little sheepishly, pulled the hoodie off over his head.

'That's great,' said Connor, surprised. 'Now the whole of Tiger Patrol is in uniform.'

'Yeah,' said Abby. 'But what's that on your back, Toby? You look like you can hardly walk!'

'It's only my rucksack,' replied Toby, swinging it off and dumping it on the ground with a thud. 'You've seen it before.'

'I know,' replied Abby. 'It was big when we went to camp, but it seems to have grown since then.'

'It's nearly as big as you are!' Andy directed his lens at the huge rucksack.

'You can laugh if you like,' said Toby. 'One day, you'll be glad I've got it.'

The car park was soon full of cars, kids and helpers. The Tigers and the Panthers piled into one minibus with Rick driving. Julie was driving the other bus with the Kestrels and the Eagles. They set off in convoy, heading for the country park.

'This looks good,' said Abby as they turned off a bypass along a single-track road and entered a large car park. Beyond, they could see woodland falling away towards a wide river estuary. 'It almost looks wild!'

'You'll probably get lost, Abby,' said Andy.

'We can't *really* get lost, can we?' Priya said, a look of alarm on her face.

Connor glanced at her. Maybe she wasn't always quite as confident as she made out, he thought. 'Andy was just kidding,' he reassured her. 'It would be pretty hard to get lost here. There are lots of walking trails around the park, and they've got signposts everywhere.'

They all piled out of the bus and joined Rick and the other patrols.

'We've got time to complete two courses here today,' he said. 'Then you'll just need the final event on the moors to get your Orienteering Badges.'

This announcement caused some excited chatter, but Rick held up a hand for silence. 'OK. This morning I want everyone to tackle a Yellow course. It's a beginner's level course, and I know some of you are keen to get on with something more challenging, but you'll find things a bit trickier here in the woods than they were in the park. And a lot of you made mistakes there, didn't you?'

Most people nodded in agreement.

'Well, now you have the chance to learn from those mistakes. You can work in the same pairs as last time. After lunch we'll complete a more difficult course in our patrols. Off you go and sign in. You collect your cards from the desk over there and then follow the red ribbons to the start.

If you do get lost, simply head for a waymarked trail and follow it back to the car park – but if you do that, make sure you go to the finish and check in, otherwise they'll think something really *has* gone wrong. Have fun!'

Connor and Priya went down to the start together. It was a beautiful autumn morning and the leaves on the trees were just starting to change colour. Connor could see the river flashing blue in the distance. This was the kind of thing he loved best – being outdoors on fine day. But he had a feeling that Priya was finding everything a bit daunting. A man and a woman, both in running gear, were waiting by the start.

'Right,' said the man, 'I'll take the stub of your card. When I say go, you go through the start gate and pick up your map. Then you copy your route onto the map, and as soon as you're ready, off you go. Woods you can run through are marked white on the map,' he added helpfully. 'Some people get in a muddle over that – they expect them to be green. Good luck! Go!'

'I'll tell you what,' Connor said as Priya hesitated. 'Why don't you copy the route? You're good at that. I'll be working out where we go first.'

Priya nodded gratefully and began to work. 'There are control points all over the place,' she remarked, looking at the master map. 'We'll have to be really careful to go to the right ones.'

'That's right,' said the woman at the start approvingly. 'It's very easy to make silly mistakes. Make sure you check that the number at the control point matches the number you need. Then you use the punch at the CP to punch the number on the card. All the punches are different, mind, so we'll know if you cheat!'

'We wouldn't!' began Connor indignantly, before he realized that the woman was joking.

'Go on,' she said. 'Enjoy yourselves.'

'OK,' said Connor to Priya, shaking his head and laughing as they set off, 'the first control is about a hundred metres down this path. I'm going to try and keep count of my paces this time.'

They found the first marker easily, nestling in a small pit beside the path. As they reached it, a man in running gear came crashing towards them out of the trees, grabbed the punch and punched his card, and, with the briefest of glances at his map and compass, set off again into the woods at top speed. Sweat was dripping from his face.

'He's not doing the Yellow course,' said Priya, looking puzzled. 'That must have been the wrong control, because it's definitely ours.'

'Actually, the courses all share some of the same points,' Connor explained. 'It's just that the harder courses tend to stay off the paths.' He suddenly felt glad that his dad had told him all this several times. It had been annoying, but at least he'd remembered it. He could see exactly why Priya was confused. 'Come on,' he said. 'We're wasting time. You work out where to go next.'

It took them nearly an hour to make their way round the fifteen control points. It was far harder than Connor had expected, even though the controls were all close to the path, and several times they overshot one by forgetting to take note of how far they'd gone. He was astonished when they arrived back at the car park and found that Jay and Toby were there before them. 'How did you manage that?' he demanded. 'I was sure no one overtook us.'

'It's Jay,' said Toby, laughing. 'He's brilliant at navigation. We got past you where the path went down to a point by the river. We went straight through the wood. And then we took another short cut just before the finish. I reckon we'll beat the other patrols easily this afternoon with Jay on our team.'

Connor suddenly wished it was him working with Toby. Last year the two of them had always been a team. But really, there was no choice. He and Toby had to partner the new recruits. And there was no way he wanted to work with Jay, even if he *was* a good navigator. Connor looked at Toby. He was a pretty ace navigator himself. Maybe he was giving Jay the credit to make him feel better. That would be just like Toby.

Andy and Abby were the last to arrive, red-faced and panting. 'It was Abby's fault,' said Andy cheerfully. 'She kept going too far and missing controls.'

'Yeah, and you were too busy filming and listening to music to stop me.'

'It was worth it,' said Andy. 'I got some terrific shots of people running through the woods. Can you believe how fast they go?'

'All back safely then?' said Connor's dad. 'I've been looking at the courses, Connor,' he continued. 'I had a quick run round the Orange course myself. It was a doddle. I reckon you lot are good enough to tackle the Light Green.'

'It can't have been *that* easy, Chris,' said Abby with a grin. 'You're a bit out of breath.'

'And muddy too,' said Andy.

'I can run just as fast as you lot,' laughed Connor's dad. 'What do you say, Connor? Are you going to try the Light Green?'

'I don't know, Dad,' replied Connor, looking

at his information sheet. 'It says here that the Orange course is "best for experienced youngsters". I'm not even sure we count as experienced yet. And the Light Green is harder.'

'I bet we can do it, Connor,' said Andy. 'Your dad thinks we can.'

'Right,' agreed Abby. 'I'm up for it.'

'That last course was too easy,' put in Jay, with a glance at Connor. 'At least, it was for me and Toby.'

'You'll be fine on the Light Green,' said Dr Sutcliff. 'You need a bit of a challenge.'

Connor flushed. He could feel the rest of his patrol watching him. He knew his dad was only trying to help, but he was just making it harder. 'What do you think?' he asked Toby.

Toby looked doubtful. 'We could have a go, but if it says it's hard, then it probably means it. We'll look pretty silly if we go wrong.'

'You won't go wrong,' said Connor's dad, standing up and stretching his lean frame. 'Hey, Rick, Julie,' he called. 'The Tigers are going to try the Light Green course. What do you think?'

'I think it's up to the Patrol Leader,' Rick said.

'Have you checked with the team?' asked Julie. 'Is everyone happy?'

Andy, Abby and Jay all agreed enthusiastically. Toby and Priya both looked at Connor.

'We've decided,' Connor said, standing up straight. 'We're going to take on the challenge. We'll do the Light Green.'

'Right,' said Toby. 'How about some lunch, then?'

CHAPTER 7

The Scouts tucked into their sandwiches, chocolate bars and fruit.

'I'm still hungry,' complained Abby when they'd finished. Rick was already packing away the empty food boxes and Abby was nibbling the chocolate carefully off her bar, trying to make it last.

Rick laughed. 'I know you'd all love to eat more,' he told them, 'and if you're lucky there might be a surprise for you later on. But eating a big meal before exercise isn't a brilliant idea. I'll expect you'll survive, Abby.'

When Abby had finally finished her chocolate bar, Tiger Patrol headed over to the check-in table.

'Well, now,' said a woman with long brown

hair tied back in a ponytail and a very suntanned face. 'Did you enjoy this morning?'

'It was great,' said Andy. 'Do you mind if I film them checking in?'

'Go ahead,' said the woman, smoothing her hair and smiling at the camera. 'Now, I expect you'll want to try an Orange course next. You'll find it quite a lot harder.'

'Well, actually we thought we'd try the Light Green,' Connor told her.

'Are you sure? It's four kilometres, and you know you'll have to find some of the controls by navigating to changes in contours. Have you done that before?'

'What does that mean?' asked Priya.

Connor was impressed by the way she was never embarrassed to ask when she didn't understand something. 'It's when you go up a hill and then it flattens out,' he told her. 'Or going along a flat bit and it gets steeper. The contour lines tell you that. We learned about it last summer.'

'Well, it's good that you want to take on the

challenge,' said the check-in woman. 'Here's your card.'

As they made their way down to the start, Connor felt as if his lunch had turned into a hard lump in his stomach. He could tell that Toby wasn't really sure about the navigation, and he knew for certain that his own wasn't good enough yet. Maybe it wasn't too late to change his mind. It would be the sensible thing to do. But then, Andy and Abby were really up for it. And he'd seen the way Jay had looked at him: Jay thought he was scared.

'Connor,' said Priya. 'Give him the card. You were miles away.'

Connor blinked and saw that they'd already arrived at the start. The man was looking up at him, smiling and holding his hand out for the card. 'Light Green, eh?' he said. 'You'll have to keep your wits about you, you know.' He tore off the stub. 'I'll start you at fourteen hundred hours. A minute from now.'

It was too late, thought Connor. He'd just

have to make the best of it. He took a deep breath. 'Priya's really good at copying the route,' he told the others. 'Can you check as she does it, Toby? The rest of us had better look at the master map and get a rough idea of where we're going.'

'The first leg is straight through the woods,' Abby said. 'It's nearly three hundred metres.'

'Right,' said Connor, feeling a little more confident. 'The control is on a path junction so we can aim to the east of it; then we'll know that when we find the path we have to go west.'

'OK,' said Priya, standing up. 'I think I'm ready. Can you set the bearing, Connor?'

Connor took the map and laid the edge of his compass along the line between the start and the first point. Then he lined up the orienting lines on the compass dial with the grid lines on the map. 'Forty degrees,' he said. 'But we'll call it fifty degrees to make sure we hit the path to the east. You take the map, Toby. Keep track of where we are.'

He held the compass in front of him. 'Up

there,' he said. 'We should aim for that tree first of all.'

Jay thought Connor was one of the most annoying people he'd ever met. Anyone could tell that he hadn't really wanted to do this course, and now he was just taking over and making a big deal out of doing all this really careful navigation stuff. He and Toby could have done it much quicker. It had been a good day up till now, apart from that one nasty moment when he'd seen Lee, Sean and Vicky all riding towards him along the pavement. He felt a little sick just thinking about it. What if they'd seen his uniform?

'Let's go,' said Abby. 'We're wasting time. It's that way.'

'Don't go too fast,' Connor called as he followed her through the trees with Priya and Andy – who stopped every so often to shoot a few seconds of video.

Toby and Jay brought up the rear. 'Is Connor always like this?' Jay asked Toby.

'Not really,' replied Toby. 'You can see what his dad is like. He always wants Connor to try the most difficult things. Like, everything Connor does, his dad's done it better when *he* was in the Scouts. And his grandpa too, Connor says.'

'I suppose my dad was a bit like that about football,' said Jay. 'But I'm useless at it. What's your dad like?'

'I've never met him,' replied Toby cheerfully. 'He left when I was a baby. My mum doesn't know anything about the Scouts either, but I bet she'd be really good at everything we do.'

'I don't think *my* mum would,' replied Jay. He felt bad, asking Toby about his dad like that. But Toby didn't seem bothered. Jay looked ahead and saw the others disappearing into the trees. 'Come on,' he said. 'We'd better hurry.'

They put on a spurt and caught up with Priya and Andy as they reached the path. 'Good,' said Connor. 'Now we go west. Let's run.'

They set off at a fast jog. Jay was glad he'd

done so much mountain biking because it was clear that the other Tigers were all very fit, especially Connor. It was surprisingly far to the path junction, but when they reached it, the control was easy to find.

'We'll have to be much more careful from now on,' Connor said. 'We can only find the next point by accurate navigation. Look, we go out of the trees and across that big grassy hillside. The control's on the top of a spur, but there are at least four spurs that look much the same.'

'Jay could take the bearing,' Toby said as Connor pored over the map. 'Go on, Connor – we should all have a turn.'

Jay could see that Connor was annoyed, but he took the map anyway and worked carefully for a few moments, with his tongue sticking out. Then he held the compass and looked up at the hillside. It was a wide, featureless, grassy slope. There wasn't a rock or a tree or anything to help him. 'There's nothing really to fix on,' he said doubtfully. 'It all looks the same.'

'We have to hurry,' Connor said, looking at his watch. 'This is all taking too long.'

'That's not my fault,' replied Jay.

'I know what we could do,' said Andy unexpectedly. 'I was reading a book about navigation. Has someone got another compass?'

'Of course,' said Toby, delving into his huge rucksack. 'I've got two. In case one of them breaks,' he added when he saw the others staring at him. 'What do you want to do, Andy?'

'Jay can go ahead,' Andy said. 'He follows the bearing and Toby sets the same bearing on his compass. We follow on behind, and Toby checks that Jay is going in the right direction.'

'OK, good,' Connor said. 'Are you ready, Jay?'

Jay nodded and held the compass out ahead of him the way Rick had shown them at their last meeting. After he'd gone about fifty metres he paused and looked back. Toby raised his arm and pointed, slightly more to the north than Jay had been heading.

Jay checked the bearing. It was very hard to be

sure if he'd been going straight. He decided Toby must be right and adjusted his course a little. He went up a steepish slope, and then the ground levelled off a little. He climbed further and the hillside steepened again. Suddenly he was at the top and could see a village in the distance, and the cars on the main road. But there was no sign of a control point.

The others came up beside him. They looked back and saw the wide river estuary below them. 'You must have gone past it,' Connor accused him.

'Well, I didn't see anything,' Jay replied. 'I was watching the compass, wasn't I? How far did we come?'

Connor looked closely at the map, and Jay saw that his face was red. Priya started to say something but Connor cut her off sharply. 'I'm not sure where we are exactly,' he continued. 'What do the rest of you think?'

Jay had to turn away to hide a smile. Connor really wasn't as great as he thought he was.

'Actually, I think we've come three hundred metres,' said Priya. 'We ought to go back a bit. The point we're looking for must be back where the slope changed the first time.'

She took the map and showed them all what she meant. There were two places where the contour lines were drawn very close together. 'That's the first steep bit,' she said, pointing. 'And the control point must be somewhere along the top of it.'

'Why didn't you say before?' asked Connor irritably.

'I tried,' Priya said, 'but you told me to be quiet.'

'Oh.' Connor flushed again. 'Sorry, Priya.'

'Well,' said Abby brightly to fill the awkward silence. 'I'm going down there. Can't we just walk along the edge of the steep bit until we find it?'

'OK,' said Connor, and Jay could hear that he was trying hard to keep his voice cheerful. 'That's what we'll do. We're just going to have to make up the time on the other legs. Let's hope it won't all be as hard as this one.'

Abby led the way back down the slope. When the ground steepened again she began walking north. She hadn't gone far before she gave a shout. 'Found it!' she yelled, and they all rushed to join her.

'Brilliant, Abby!' said Andy, raising his camcorder to get a shot of her standing triumphantly by the control.

'That's good,' said Connor. 'But if we take this long on every control we'll still be here at midnight.'

'Well, we'll just have to get better,' said Priya. 'This one was hard, but we found it eventually, didn't we?'

Jay was surprised that Priya was still talking to Connor after the way he'd snapped at her. She actually seemed to like him.

'Go on, Andy,' said Connor. 'You do the navigation for the next one. Priya can hold your camera for you.'

Andy laughed. 'OK, then,' he said, handing over the camera. 'Don't . . .'

'Drop it,' said Priya, finishing his sentence for him. 'Don't worry, I won't.'

Connor forced himself to concentrate as they worked their way round the rest of the course. He knew he had a short fuse, and he felt really bad for shouting at Priya. It hadn't been her fault at all. Now he worked hard to make sure they all took turns to lead, and navigate, and count steps. Even so, they got lost several more times, and when they finally arrived at the finish the officials were getting ready to pack up.

'Well done,' they said as Connor handed over the completed card. 'It looks like you got them all, but you'd better hurry. Your Scout Leader was down here a few minutes ago looking for you. I think they're ready to leave.'

Connor followed the other weary Tigers back up the path to the car park. It had been difficult – even more tricky than he'd expected – but he couldn't help feeling pleased that they'd completed the course. And everyone had helped. Even Jay, he had to admit.

They trudged into the car park and found the minibuses loaded and ready to depart. A worried-looking Rick was deep in conversation with Connor's dad. Their faces both broke into relieved smiles when they saw the Tigers approaching.

'Well?' Rick said to Connor as the others climbed into the bus. 'Did you finish the course?'

'In the end,' replied Connor. 'It was hard. We . . . well, we got lost a few times.'

'You should have been back here by four p.m. We were starting to worry.'

'I know,' said Connor. 'I'm sorry, Rick. We were as quick as we could be.'

'Well, we've had to wait half an hour for you, and you know that Scouts are supposed to think about other people.' Rick paused, then smiled. 'Still, I'm pleased you did it. And the good thing is, all the other helpers had time to get back before us and set up the barbecue. By the time we return the burgers should be ready.' He patted Connor on the back and climbed into the driving seat.

He was right. They arrived back at Scout HQ to the mouth-watering smell of juicy burgers and sausages sizzling over the fire. After the hours of walking, the Scouts were grateful for hot food. Their eyes lit up when they saw the plate of baked bananas stuffed with marshmallows and covered in chocolate sauce.

'Hey, Tigers,' said Andy. 'I want to take a picture.' He pulled a small camera out of his rucksack and balanced it on a table. He arranged the Tigers in a group, all holding steaming bananas, then pressed a button on the camera and ran to join them. They all held up bananas and cheered as the camera clicked.

They gathered round to laugh at the picture. There was Priya, with her long black hair and her uniform still as perfect as they'd been at the start of the day, and Abby looking as wild as always.

Jay and Toby were both laughing at the camera, and Andy was on the end looking like a man of mystery. Connor himself stood in the middle, tanned, taller than the others, with a huge smile on his face.

It was funny, he thought, but they actually looked like a team. They'd done something hard and they'd done it together.

He hoped it was going to last.

CHAPTER 8

Jay woke up on a Saturday morning two weeks later and knew that it was a special day, but for a few moments he couldn't remember *why* it was special. Then it came back to him – today was the day of the massive orienteering event. They were actually going out onto the moors, into proper wild countryside. He had a quick shower, and then dressed in his uniform.

As he was leaving his room, he caught sight of himself in the mirror. That Scout was him! He smiled. He wouldn't have believed he could get used to it so quickly, but the last two Scout meetings had been a lot of fun. He didn't think he'd ever get on with Connor, not really, but the others were great. It was a shame they didn't go to his school. If they'd been there, he wouldn't have to worry so much about Lee and Vicky and Sean. They never actually *did* anything at school – just followed him around and yelled things at him. But he knew that one day they'd get him on his own, and then . . .

I don't have to think about that today, he told himself. *Today's going to be a good day*.

He ran downstairs. 'You look very smart, love,' said his mum approvingly. 'What is it you're doing, exactly?'

'We're going to the moors,' Jay said. 'We have to find our way around using a map and a compass.'

'Sounds very exciting, doesn't it, Harry?'

'Stumbling around on those moors?' said Jay's dad. 'Not for me, love. I'm off to the match this afternoon.'

'Now, then,' his mum said. 'You'll need a nice big breakfast. Eat your cereal, and the bacon and eggs will be ready in a minute. I expect you'll have a long day.'

'It'll be worth it,' Jay told her. 'If we complete

the course then I'll get my Orienteering Badge. It'll be my first one.'

'I thought you weren't interested in badges,' said his mum, smiling.

'Yeah, well, I'm not really. It's just . . .'

'Don't worry!' laughed his mum. 'I'm teasing. You are allowed to change your mind, you know.'

There was a knock on the door just as Jay was finishing his breakfast. 'That'll be Toby,' he said, getting up. 'He told me he'd call for me on the way.'

Toby came into the room with his enormous rucksack on his back. It seemed even bigger than before, although Jay wasn't sure that was possible.

'What have you got in there?' asked Jay's dad with a smile. 'The kitchen sink?'

'I didn't mean to bring quite so much,' Toby admitted. 'But I kept thinking of things we might need, and I ended up with quite a lot of stuff. It's all useful, honestly.'

Jay picked up his own rucksack, which he'd packed carefully the night before. Even when he'd added the lunch his mum handed him, and a big bottle of water, it was still only half the size of Toby's.

'Have a great time, boys,' Jay's mum called after them as they set off down the street together.

Jay was chatting so excitedly to Toby about the day ahead that he didn't even bother to check whether Lee and the gang were around.

Connor had woken up feeling as if he was about to take a test at school. Then, like Jay, he remembered that this was the day of the big orienteering event. He went downstairs and found his dad and his grandpa already eating their breakfast. His grandparents had driven down from Manchester the night before. His grandpa taught at the university, but his main reason for living there was so that he could spend all his spare time walking and climbing in the hills. He wasn't as tall as Connor's dad, but he was lean and fit.

'Tuck in, Connor,' he said. 'I've made you my

special porridge. You've got a big day ahead of you. I hope Tiger Patrol's going to win.'

'It's not a competition, Grandpa,' Connor said. 'The main thing is, we all get our badges if we complete the course.'

'What do you mean, *if*?' demanded his dad. 'You'll have no trouble. Not after all the practice we've done. And I bet the Tigers *will* be the best.'

Connor ate his porridge in silence. His dad had discovered that there was a permanent orienteering course set up in some woods about thirty miles away, and he'd driven Connor over there the previous weekend. They'd spent the whole day navigating through the woods in the rain. Connor supposed that it had been useful, but it had also been very cold and wet, and by the time they'd finished his head had been reeling with all the things his dad had been trying to explain to him. He'd felt as if his navigation was getting worse, not better. He told himself not to worry so much. At least the sun was shining this morning. And there was another good thing too. All the Tigers seemed to be getting on well together – even Jay.

'Penny for them,' said his grandpa, smiling.

'Oh . . . I was just thinking it's a good job it's a nice day, Grandpa. It would be horrible to be out on the moors in weather like we had last weekend.'

'Ah,' said his grandpa. 'You might need my special survival cakes. I baked them last night after you'd gone to bed.' He produced a plastic box containing two foil-wrapped packages. 'Full of goodness,' he added. 'And they taste good too!'

'Hey, thanks, Grandpa.'

'See,' said his dad. 'You've got everything you need! Are you ready? Let's go.'

Down at Scout HQ, the two minibuses were waiting. Other Scouts had begun to arrive and were talking excitedly in little groups. Toby and Jay were standing with Priya, who was showing them a new compass.

'My dad bought it for me,' she said. 'He told me he didn't want me getting lost on the moors.'

'What's that?' Connor asked Toby, staring at his gigantic rucksack. 'Are you going on an expedition to Everest?'

They all laughed. 'Toby says that it's all useful,' Jay said. 'He's probably got a laptop in there.'

'I haven't, actually,' Toby replied. 'I don't really trust electronic gadgets in the wilderness. They can get broken, and batteries can run out, and—'

'Toby!' laughed Connor. 'We're not going to the wilderness. What *have* you brought?'

'Well,' began Toby, 'there's my—'

But before he could say another word Andy's dad pulled up, and Abby and Andy jumped out. 'We're not late, are we?' asked Andy. 'Rick said I should give Dad a bit of help, so I did.'

'He did everything but drive the car.' Andy's dad grinned; he seemed to have forgotten to comb his hair and was wearing odd socks. 'He seems to think this is some kind of important occasion. Abby does too. She was knocking on the door at a quarter to eight.'

'Just in case Andy forgot to set the alarm,' laughed Abby.

'Oh yeah? Like I'd do that,' retorted Andy indignantly.

'Well, see you, kids,' said Mr Mackenzie. 'Have a great day. Don't get lost!'

They all groaned. 'That's not funny, Dad,' said Andy as his dad started the engine.

'No,' agreed Abby. 'But I'll tell you what *is* funny. You've left your rucksack in the car.'

'Dad!' Andy yelled, waving madly and running after the car. 'Stop!'

He returned red-faced a few moments later with a bulky rucksack slung over his shoulder. 'You should have reminded me,' he said to Abby.

'Sorry,' Abby replied with a straight face. 'I didn't think you'd need reminding. You have such a good memory and you're so well organized . . .'

The others all burst out laughing, and after a moment even Andy joined in. Then they heard Rick's voice calling them together.

'I'd like each Patrol Leader to collect a box of equipment for your patrol. Then you can share it out. There are pens, paper, compasses and some spare bottles of water, and there's a first-aid kit for each group, which I hope you won't need. Sort yourselves out as fast as you can and then we can get going.'

'This is it, then, Connor,' said his dad as he walked over to the stores. 'Your team all look in good form. Grandpa's coming up later to watch you finish. And don't forget the things we were practising.'

'I won't, Dad,' Connor said. 'You don't have to keep reminding me, you know.'

He knew his dad meant well, but sometimes he wished he'd just leave him alone.

Jay waited with the others while Connor collected the equipment. 'It feels like a real expedition, doesn't it?' Priya said to him. 'Our first since we joined officially.'

'Yeah, it's good,' Jay answered, a little

embarrassed. The four new Scouts had all made their promises the previous week. 'Have you been out on the moors before?'

'I came with my dad and my brother once,' Priya replied. 'But actually, we didn't go very far. I always think it looks kind of scary out there. All those rocks and heather and no houses anywhere.'

'It's not so bad,' Jay replied. 'Especially not on a sunny day like this. I came last year, when I was still at primary school. We went on a bird-watching trip and we saw buzzards and kestrels and curlews. It was great.'

'Yeah, but that's different from going out there on our own, isn't it?' Priya said.

'I guess,' Jay began. 'I came another time to go biking, but that was with my dad—'

Then he stopped. A voice echoed across the car park – a voice that Jay recognized only too well: 'Hi, Jay. What are you doing?'

It was Lee. Several of Lee's mates were with him. They were all standing astride their bikes at the edge of the car park. Vicky suddenly stood up on the pedals and rode her bike directly towards where Tiger Patrol were standing. Jay felt his face reddening and he knew that all the Scouts and helpers had turned to see what was going on.

Vicky skidded to a halt in front of him. 'You're wearing a uniform!' she said at last. 'Hey, everyone, look at little Jay! He's wearing a uniform. It's really pretty, Jay – especially that scarf thingy. What are you, a baby soldier?'

'We're Scouts,' said Connor, who had recognized Vicky from the time in the park. 'What's wrong with that?'

'Oooh!' she squealed. 'Scouts! Hey, everyone,' she called to her friends, 'we've found the Boy Scouts. Little Jay's a Boy Scout.'

'Actually, we're just Scouts,' Priya said. 'You can be a boy or a girl. Anyone can join. You could if you wanted.'

'Shut up, Priya,' said Jay. 'You'll just make them worse.'

'Hey, Lee,' said Vicky. 'You want to be a Scout? This kid says we can join.'

'Nah,' said Lee, inspecting Jay's uniform with his hard blue eyes. 'I'll give it a miss, thanks. Where are you all off to, then? Going camping?'

'No, actually,' said Connor; his jaw hardened and he stood tall. 'We're going to Carrick Moor. We're going orienteering.'

'You're mad,' Lee said. 'Specially you, Jay. Scouts is just for saddos. I always knew you were a loser.'

'You lot,' called Julie, coming out of the building. 'This is a private car park, so you can take yourselves out of here right now.'

'You what?' said Lee rudely.

'You heard me,' replied Julie, pointing.

'You can't tell us what to do, just 'cos you've got a uniform on. It doesn't mean anything, does it?'

Julie shrugged and took her phone from her pocket. 'I'll call the police if you like. Your choice.'

After a few moments Lee and Vicky turned and rode their bikes back across the tarmac, doing wheelies as they went. At the edge of the car park they stopped.

'Hey, Jay!' called Lee. 'Maybe we'll come and watch you.'

Jay's face was sullen and miserable. He turned away.

'They're the same ones, aren't they?' asked Toby. 'The ones who were in the park that morning when we were orienteering.' He turned to the others. 'They go to Jay's school.'

'Big deal,' said Priya. 'They're just a bunch of bullies. You should ignore them, Jay.'

'We'll *all* ignore them,' Julie said as Rick joined them.

'Trouble?' he asked, looking after the retreating gang.

'Nothing I couldn't deal with,' replied Julie with a smile. 'Let's get into the minibuses. It's time we were on our way.'

Jay climbed aboard and slumped in the nearest

seat. He put his head in his hands. Why had he been so stupid? He'd walked all the way from home wearing his uniform, forgetting to keep a lookout. They must have spotted him and followed him, and now he knew they would never leave him alone.

'Hey, Jay,' said Priya, plopping down in the seat beside him. 'You know, they're really stupid, that lot. Who cares what they think?'

Jay didn't reply. He turned away and looked out of the window. The gang were still there, laughing and calling out. Priya stood up and Toby took her place. He snapped his seatbelt on and the minibus moved off. Jay heard a thud and a clatter as something hit the back of the minibus. He looked back and saw a couple of cans and a plastic bottle rolling in the gutter. The gang were still jeering as they turned the corner and headed for the moors.

'Just forget about them,' Toby said. 'We're going to have a good time, right? You're the best map-reader in the whole troop, so I reckon Tiger Patrol could finish first.'

'I couldn't care less,' said Jay. 'It's all a total waste of time.'

'No, it's not,' Toby insisted. 'We've been learning loads of really useful stuff doing orienteering – you know we have.'

'Yeah, well, I'm sick of it,' muttered Jay. 'I never wanted to be in the stupid Scouts in the first place.'

He turned to the window and wouldn't say another word to Toby. He felt even worse than he had before because he knew it wasn't true, what he'd said to Toby. He liked the Scouts, but he was scared. Next week was half term, but after that he had to go back to school. He'd have to face Lee and Vicky and all the rest of them, and he knew they'd never leave him alone now. He was dreading seeing them again – they were going to make his life hell.

CHAPTER 9

Connor gazed out of the window as the minibus laboured up the steep hill out of town. The houses came to an end quite suddenly and the main road snaked on ahead of them over the open moor. He glanced across at Jay, but he was still slumped moodily in his seat. Connor was annoyed about what had just happened – he felt as if the whole day had been spoiled. First his dad going on at him, now this.

In the seat behind him, Andy and Abby were talking. 'Do you know where we're going, exactly?' Andy asked.

'I never really paid much attention to the moors,' Abby replied. 'When you drive over them to go to the city for shopping they don't look that interesting. And when it's all cloudy up there, it's just creepy.'

Connor turned round and looked at them. Andy and Abby always made him feel better. 'It's quite high up,' he told them. 'There's a car park where a stream comes down off the hills. Up there – look.'

The minibus slowed down, and they turned off onto a narrow side-road that climbed steadily uphill between heather and rocks. They rumbled over a cattle-grid, and almost at once they had to slow down as some sheep wandered slowly in front of them. Ahead, Connor saw the orange and white orienteering sign fluttering in the breeze at the entrance to the car park. Rick pulled in, and the other minibus drew up beside them.

The Scouts all piled out, but Jay remained in his seat.

'I tried talking to him,' Toby said to Connor.

'Me too,' said Priya. 'He's in a really bad mood.'

Connor watched as Rick went and spoke to

Jay. After a few moments Jay climbed out and walked reluctantly over to join them.

'Good,' said Rick. 'We're ready to start. But before we do, I want to remind you all about the rules. It's a long way between controls on this course, so you need to take extra care, and . . .'

Connor glanced across at Jay. He was staring at the ground angrily, paying no attention to anyone. Connor could see why he had been upset, but it was over now. Jay looked like he had when he'd first started at Scouts. He was going to mess everything up for the rest of them.

'Is that clear, everyone?' said Rick.

Connor realized guiltily that he hadn't been paying attention.

'OK,' Rick continued. 'We're all doing the same course, and we'll be setting off at fifteen-minute intervals. Once we've registered, we'll draw lots to see which order we start in. When it's time to go, you can make your way down to the start. It works just the same way as the last event. You'll be started off, and then you transfer your course from the master map to your own maps. I'd like you *all* to do that today, so that each of you has a copy of the map. As soon as you've done it, then you're away. It's a long course, but you should all be back here by two p.m. Now, off you go and register.'

At the check-in desk Connor was surprised to see the same ponytailed, suntanned woman from the previous event. 'I remember you,' she said with a grin. 'Tiger Patrol, isn't it? You nearly made me late for my tea last time.'

'We didn't mean to,' began Connor. 'We did the course as fast as we could, but—'

'Hey, it's OK,' the woman said, smiling. 'You weren't that late. You did really well getting round that course. Let's hope you do just as well today, eh? Here's your card.'

Connor took the card, feeling a little foolish.

'Here,' said Rick, holding out his hat. 'Pick a number. Lowest number goes first. Highest goes last.'

Connor pulled out the number four. There

were four patrols, so Tiger Patrol would be setting off last of all.

'You can explore up behind the car park while you wait,' Rick told them. 'Just don't go out of sight. You'll be starting at eleven.'

They collected their rucksacks, Jay trailing sullenly behind them, and carried them a little way up the hillside to where a stream tumbled down in a rocky bed. The sun was surprisingly warm, despite the high, wispy clouds that were spreading across the sky. Andy, Abby and Priya made their way up the stream bed, laughing together. Jay sat on a rock looking miserable.

'Don't worry about him,' Toby said to Connor. 'Once we get going I bet he'll start to enjoy himself.'

'What, so we're just going to do everything for him?' said Connor. 'We'd be better off leaving him behind at the start, if you ask me. He's going to slow us down.'

'No one's ever picked on you at school, have they?' said Toby, looking sharply at his friend.

Connor shook his head. 'Not really,' he said.

'Well, you know I've been bullied,' Toby continued. 'Remember that time those boys from Year Ten had me in the cloakroom and you came in?'

'Yeah, but that was just one time,' Connor said. He glanced at Toby. 'Wasn't it?'

'Not really. There were plenty of other times when you *weren't* around. Some people think it's weird to like maths and science and not really care about football.'

'You never said anything.'

Toby shrugged. 'What difference would that have made? You weren't going to follow me around all the time, were you? I sorted it out myself.'

Connor looked at the small and wiry Toby. Suddenly he had a feeling that Toby would make a bad enemy and he wondered exactly *how* he had sorted it out.

'All I'm saying is,' Toby continued, 'you can't blame Jay for being fed up. I know exactly how he feels. That lot have really got it in for him. You could see.'

'I suppose,' said Connor. 'But he doesn't have to take it out on us, does he?'

Toby didn't reply. He stood up. 'We should check that everyone's got everything,' he said. 'Just to make sure. I've got a feeling the weather might change.'

Connor was annoyed with himself. He'd been so worried about Jay that he hadn't been doing his job properly. He called the others back and checked that everyone had waterproofs and food and a compass. Jay had a first-aid kit, and Connor had a mobile phone.

'OK, I think we're ready,' he said finally. And then he had an idea. He delved into his rucksack and produced one of his grandpa's cakes.

'What is it?' asked Abby as he undid the foil wrapping. 'It looks like some sort of breakfast bar.'

The cake was golden brown, full of grains and pieces of fruit. 'My grandpa's special survival rations,' Connor said. 'I thought we could all

have a bit before we start. Hold on, I'll cut it up.'
He felt in his pocket and pulled out his knife.

'Hey,' said Toby, watching the razor-sharp blade slice up small squares. 'Where did you get that?'

'From my dad,' said Connor as he handed out pieces of cake. Only Jay refused one, sitting sullenly on his rock. 'It was my grandpa's originally. I think it's quite old.'

'They started making them like this in 1961,' Toby said, examining the knife as he chewed his lump of cake. 'The history of Swiss Army knives is very interesting. Although this is actually a *soldier*'s knife. They had—'

They all burst out laughing. 'Only *you* would know stuff like that, Toby,' Abby said, with her mouth full.

They'd only just finished when they heard Rick calling: it was time to make their way down to the start.

'Here you are,' said the official at the start gate. 'A map for each of you. As soon as you hear the beep you can go through and start copying your route. Your Troop Leader tells me you're experienced, so you're tackling the Green course. Good luck!'

The beep sounded and they rushed through the gate. They each set to work locating the control points on their list on the master map and then transferring them carefully to their own maps.

Connor looked up and saw that Jay was doing nothing. 'Hey, come on, Jay.' He remembered what Toby had said and tried to keep the irritation he was feeling out of his voice. 'You know Rick said we all had to carry a map.'

'What's the point? You've all got one, haven't you?'

'We have to do this properly,' Connor insisted. 'We're going out on the moor and everyone should have a map.' He didn't care if Jay was upset. He knew they had to follow the rules.

'Yeah? Well, you do what you like. You can go and tell Rick I won't follow orders if you want.'

'Don't worry, Connor,' said Toby. 'I've done two. Here . . .'

He held the map out to Jay, and for a moment Connor thought Jay was going to crumple it up and chuck it away, but then he stuffed it into his pocket.

'OK, then,' Connor said. 'Priya, why don't you do the bearing for the first checkpoint? It looks as if we can go straight over the moor.'

'I've already done it,' she replied with a grin. 'You can all set it on your compasses. Two hundred and seventy-five degrees.'

They all stood up and slipped their maps back into their plastic wallets. Priya pointed up the gently rising hillside as the others – except Jay – set their bearings. 'We go over the top of that,' she said, 'and the control is on a rocky outcrop. It's about three hundred metres away.'

'We should work out how long it's going to take us to get there,' Toby said. 'Jay, you're good at that.'

Jay ignored him.

'OK, then,' Toby went on. 'I'll do it. It's four kilometres an hour, so that's one point five minutes for each hundred metres we walk, plus a minute for each ten metres we climb. I'll just count the contours—'

'We're wasting time,' Andy said impatiently. 'We can easily estimate when we've walked three hundred metres, can't we? And it's sunny. We can see where were going.'

'I'm just being careful,' Toby replied. 'It won't take long. Next time, one of us should be doing this while someone else is taking the bearing. There! If we walk for ten minutes we should be somewhere near the control.'

'Let's go, then,' said Connor, and with a glance at his compass he led the way into the heather.

They climbed steadily up the low hill, with Jay trailing slowly behind them. When they reached the top, they saw several outcrops of rock ahead of them and paused for a moment.

Priya checked her compass and pointed ahead. 'It's that one there, don't you think?'

They all agreed, and Priya was about to march off again, but Connor turned and saw that Jay was still walking very slowly up the hill. 'We'd better wait,' he said reluctantly.

'The weather's definitely changing,' Toby said. 'Look over there.'

Away to the west, a band of cloud was spreading across the sky. It hadn't been there five minutes before.

'Hurry up, Jay,' Connor said as Jay finally reached them. 'It'll take us all day at this rate.'

Jay shrugged. 'You don't have to wait for me,' he said.

'Yeah, well, we do, actually.' Connor was unable to stop the anger creeping into his voice. 'We have to go at the speed of the slowest member of the party. That's what Rick told us. We're heading for those rocks there,' he added, pointing. 'Let's see if we can get there a bit quicker this time.'

They headed off once more, but by the time they reached the rocks and Priya had triumphantly found their first control point, Jay was still a hundred metres behind them. Connor took out the card and punched the first box.

'Don't worry about it, Connor,' Andy said. 'We'll do the next bearing and work out where to go, and by the time Jay gets here we'll be ready to start.'

He pulled out his map and compass and started work. When he'd taken the bearing, he held up the compass and gazed ahead. Over to their left the land fell away slightly. There was a track running through the heather, and beyond it was rough, tussocky grass and then trees. Directly ahead was heathery moorland that seemed to stretch on to the horizon. 'We go up,' he said. 'It's another three-hundred-metre leg and the control is on a bridge over a small stream. Should be easy.'

In the distance they saw a small figure running, silhouetted for a moment against the sky. Then it disappeared over the top of the hill and the moors were empty again.

'I know there are grown-ups checking up on us,' Priya said, 'but it does seem kind of lonely out here.'

They all looked around. There wasn't another person to be seen, or a house. The sun suddenly went behind a cloud, and instantly they all felt cold.

'We have to keep moving,' Connor said, shivering. 'We can't keep stopping like this.' He turned back. 'Jay!' he called. 'Get a move on!'

Jay stopped. 'You can't tell me what to do,' he said.

Connor felt his face getting hot. He really wanted to make a good job of this task after the way things had gone on the last one. He'd spent all last weekend getting cold and wet with his dad, and he was pretty sure Jay had spent it in front of a computer screen. 'You're just acting like a big baby,' he shouted angrily. 'Just because a few stupid kids had a go at you, you're taking it out on us. It's not fair.'

Jay stared at him for a moment. 'I told you,' he

said. 'You can do it without me. If you think I'm following you around all day, then you're crazy. You do your stupid course and get your stupid badges. I'm off.'

And with that he pulled off his scarf, threw it on the ground, then turned and raced away through the heather.

CHAPTER 10

Connor stared after Jay. His heart was beating fast and his hands were trembling. 'Hey, come back, you idiot!' he yelled. 'We're not supposed to go that way. Jay! Stop!'

He took a few steps down the hillside after Jay and then stopped, but he could still hear the others talking about him.

'Why did Connor yell at him like that?' Abby hissed at Toby. 'What's going on?'

'Connor never shouts,' Andy said disbelievingly. 'Jay was being a pain, but who cares if we go a bit slowly?'

'Can't we just go after him?' asked Priya, stooping to pick up Jay's discarded scarf.

'Maybe we should,' said Toby. 'Jay's all right really. I bet if we catch him he'll come with us. But we'd better be quick or he'll be out of sight.'

Connor forced himself to turn and face them, his hands clenched by his side. 'We can't go after him,' he said grimly. 'We have to find an adult and tell them what's happened.'

'But we can't leave Jay out here on his own,' said Abby. 'You wouldn't like it if we left you, Connor.'

'I wouldn't run off in a stupid temper,' replied Connor, feeling himself growing angry again.

'Well, I still say we can't leave him,' Abby repeated stubbornly. 'I don't care what you think.'

'Stop it, you two,' said Andy. 'Listen, Connor, if we catch up with Jay we'll hardly have lost any time at all. No one can see us from here, can they? We're completely out of sight of any of the checkpoints, and they'll all think we're just not very good at navigating, like last time.'

'But we'll have to be quick,' Abby said. 'Come on, Connor. I bet he'll just go a little way and then stop.'

Connor shook his head. 'I don't know,' he said. 'I'm sure we ought to get help, but . . .'

Thoughts were racing around his head. He could just imagine what his dad would say if they trailed back to the checkpoint missing one member of the patrol. They'd probably have to call the whole event off if someone was lost, and it would all be his fault. It was his fault. He knew it was. He should never have lost his temper with Jay. But what the others said was true. If they could just find Jay and bring him back, there'd be plenty of time to complete the course and no one would ever know.

'Connor,' said Priya anxiously. 'What are we going to do?'

He blinked. They'd been standing here far too long. 'We'll go after him,' he said. 'But—'

'Come on, then,' said Abby, setting off down the hillside. 'If we don't get a move on we'll lose him.'

She was like a deer, racing away from them. The others followed after, leaping over clumps of heather and rocks and yelling Jay's name.

Connor trailed behind them. He'd messed everything up, and now he wasn't even leading his own patrol. None of them were paying any attention to him and he couldn't really blame them. Lost in his own gloomy thoughts, he crossed over the track and followed the others across a patch of open grassland.

'Here's a footprint!' called Priya. 'He definitely came this way.'

Just as she said it, Connor's foot slipped off a clump of grass and squelched deep into the mud. He looked around and saw that there were patches of bright green moss between the grassy tussocks, and in places he noticed the glint of water. 'Be careful, everyone,' he called. 'It's very wet here. It could even be boggy.'

He caught up with the others and found them looking down at the footprint in the mud. 'It's new,' Toby said. 'It's definitely Jay's.'

They looked ahead. The wet grassy stuff continued for a few hundred metres, but then the land rose a little and there were some small trees.

'Here's another footprint,' said Abby, going on ahead. 'He's definitely come this way. He's probably hiding in those trees. Hurry up, you lot! What are you waiting for?'

'Try not to get too wet,' Connor said. They were all struggling across the marshy ground.

'You're joking,' replied Toby as he put his foot on a solid-looking piece of grass and went in up to his knee.

It was the same for all of them. By the time they had struggled back to solid ground they all had dripping trousers and boots. When Andy took out his camcorder to film them, even Abby didn't think it was very funny.

'You can't,' she said. 'Not now. We'll have to keep moving or we'll get cold. And we'd better find Jay quickly.'

'You go on ahead,' Andy said. 'I have to get some footage of this marshy stuff. We can show it to other people and they'll know what to look out for, won't they? I mean, it looks just like ordinary grass from here.'

They all looked back. It was true, thought Connor. You couldn't see how wet it was until you were in the middle.

'That moss is a great clue,' Andy said. 'I'll make sure I get some good shots of that.'

Abby sighed and turned to Connor. 'There's no stopping him when he's thinking about movie-making,' she said.

Connor looked at his watch. Time seemed to be passing incredibly quickly. It was already a quarter to twelve.

'Go on,' Andy said. 'I'll run and catch you up in a minute.'

'Well, OK,' said Connor. 'But hurry.'

He strode on up the gentle slope, passing between the first small trees. None of the others seemed to understand how serious this was. They'd lost a team member, and now Andy wanted to hang around taking pictures – and Abby seemed to think it was OK. This was all a terrible mistake. He should never have let them talk him into it. They should have gone straight to a checkpoint and told someone what had happened. Where *was* Jay? He couldn't have gone much further surely?

'Hey!' said Andy, running up beside him. 'I got some great shots, Connor. And I took some more of you lot walking up through the trees. I told you I'd catch up.'

They walked on steadily for nearly a quarter of an hour, calling Jay's name from time to time. At last Connor halted. There were trees all around them now. The others came up and stood around in a circle.

'We're going downhill again,' Toby said.

'How are we going to find Jay in this lot?' asked Andy. 'He could be anywhere.' Suddenly their search seemed completely hopeless.

'I don't like this much,' said Priya.

Connor saw the worry on her face, and heard it in her voice. It suddenly hit him that all the others were his responsibility. That was what being Patrol Leader meant. He'd got some things wrong today, but there was no point in feeling sorry for himself. What mattered now was to start getting things right.

'We'll spread out,' he told them. 'We can form a long line and make sure we can see the people on either side of us. That way we'll cover more ground. And we can call Jay's name. He can't have gone far, can he?'

'I never thought he would have got as far as this,' Toby said.

'You go on one end of the line, Toby,' said Connor, 'and I'll go this side. We'll keep going for ten minutes, OK? But after that, well, we'll have to decide what to do.'

They all looked at each other. 'Connor's right,' said Toby. 'We can't go on looking for ever, not on our own. If we can't find Jay now, we'll have no choice. We'll have to go back without him and get help.'

'You go next to me, Priya,' Connor said. 'I won't let you out of my sight, OK?'

Priya nodded gratefully, and Connor headed

off to his left, looking back as he went to make sure that he could still see her. They all moved slowly forward through the trees, calling Jay's name.

The ten minutes were nearly up, and they were still going gently downhill, when Connor heard Andy's voice. 'Over here!' he called. 'I've found him.'

Connor raced through the wood, with Priya following behind him, ignoring the branches that slashed at his face, the snapping dry branches beneath his feet. 'Where are you?' he called.

'Here!' yelled Andy from somewhere to his right.

He changed direction and saw Toby coming towards him. Toby pointed, and Connor spotted Abby standing by a fallen tree trunk. Jay was sitting there with his head in his hands. Andy was crouched by his side, talking to him.

Connor felt anger surging up inside him again. 'Get up, Jay,' he yelled. 'We can't hang around. We've wasted ages looking for you, and everyone's wet, and—'

He stopped. Jay looked up at him and Connor saw that he had been crying. Toby put a hand on Connor's arm and pulled him away.

'We haven't got time for this,' said Connor in a low voice, with a glance at Jay and Andy.

'I know,' said Toby, fiddling with his complicated watch. 'It's twelve fifteen already. It's taken us an hour and a quarter and we've only done one control point. The whole course is only meant to take two and a half hours.'

Connor looked at his friend and saw that Toby was just as worried as he was. 'You can see Jay's really miserable,' Toby went on. 'But I know he'll come with us. Just give him a minute or two.'

'You should talk to him – you're his friend.'

'Andy's doing OK,' replied Toby. 'I know he'd cheer *me* up if I was miserable. We should try and work out what to do next. Abby's keeping close to Priya.'

'Well, all right, then,' said Connor. He pulled out his map. 'Do you know where we are?'

'I . . . I wasn't checking where we were going,' Toby said, looking at his own map. 'Were you?'

Connor flushed. 'I was thinking about everything else,' he said.

'Well, when we set off after Jay, we were here.' Toby pointed to his map. 'Then we came roughly in this direction. Oh . . .'

'What is it?' asked Connor, hearing the edge in Toby's voice.

'This is the track we crossed, and look – everything this side of it is shaded purple. It's out of bounds, Connor. We shouldn't be here. Rick told us, back at the car park.'

When I wasn't listening, Connor thought. He looked at the purple shading. There were no features marked on that part of the map. No marsh. No woods. No contours. 'We'll just have to try going back the way we came,' he said. 'We were heading west, so we just go eastwards, over there.' He pointed. 'Once we find that marshy bit we can get back on the moors.'

He took out his compass and stared at it. 'I

don't get it . . .' he said after a moment. 'East is over there, isn't it?' he asked Toby. 'I think there must be something wrong with this.'

He shook the compass and watched the needle settle. He rotated it until the red end of the needle was over the red arrow in the base of the compass. There was no doubt about it. The direction which Connor had thought was east was actually north.

Toby took out his own compass, and the needle was pointing in exactly the same direction. He checked the compass on his watch. 'It's not the compasses,' he said. 'It's us. Maybe we haven't been walking west at all. We might even have been walking round in circles.'

Connor felt a cold shiver run down his spine, but Toby was speaking again.

'Wait,' he said, opening his rucksack. 'It's OK. I've got a real map in here.'

He unzipped a pocket and took out a pink-covered Ordnance Survey map. 'We can work it out easily,' he said. 'These are the moors here. I'm sure I can figure it out.'

Connor felt relief wash over him. Without Toby they'd have been in real trouble. You could always count on him. He looked over at the fallen tree, where Andy was still talking to Jay in a low voice. He couldn't hear what they were saying, but at least Jay was talking now.

'Just leave me alone,' said Jay. He felt stupid. He knew they'd all seen that he'd been crying. He knew he'd been crazy to run off like that. He couldn't believe how angry he'd been. Now he just felt flat and empty.

'You can't stay here,' said Andy. 'No one knows where you are and it's a long way back. We should all stay together.'

'I'll be OK. It's not that far.'

'Huh,' said Andy. 'I don't think you realize how fast you run. Me and Abby are fast, but you're faster. It took us ages to get here.' He grinned. 'Still, at least I got some good footage because of it.'

Jay smiled, despite himself.

'And anyway,' Andy continued, 'you've done all that work to get your badge. You might as well have it, even if you never come to Scouts again.'

'I suppose,' said Jay eventually. He'd expected them all to be mad at him, but Andy didn't seem mad at all. Priya and Abby were sitting nearby and they both smiled at him. Jay was puzzled by the mud caked on the team's clothes and wondered what had happened. He saw Connor and Toby talking earnestly nearby.

'Connor was only doing his best,' Andy said, following Jay's gaze. 'I know he gets worked up sometimes, but he doesn't mean it, you know. Look, here's your scarf. Priya picked it up. Are you ready?'

Jay nodded, and pulled his scarf on over his head.

'Great,' said Andy, getting to his feet. 'Hey, everyone. We're ready to go. What is it? What's up, Toby.'

They were all staring at their Assistant Patrol Leader. He stood up, pointing to the map. 'These woods go on for miles,' he said, and they could all hear the panic in his voice. 'We could be anywhere. We're lost.'

CHAPTER 11

Jay felt his heart thumping.

'What do you mean?' said Andy. 'We can't be lost. We only came from just over there.' He waved his hand vaguely in the direction he imagined they'd come from.

'Over where?' asked Toby.

'I thought it was that way,' said Abby, with a glance at Andy, 'wasn't it?' She was pointing in a completely different direction.

'We can't go anywhere,' Toby said grimly. 'Not until we work out where we are now. I don't suppose any of you happened to pay attention to where we were going?'

They all looked at each other. Abby shook her head. 'I was just thinking about catching up with Jay,' she said, embarrassed.

'How about you, Priya?' asked Connor.

She bit her lip. 'I'm really sorry,' she said. 'I was like the rest of you. I just didn't think.'

'It's OK,' Connor said. 'It's not your fault.'

There was a moment's silence. Jay knew what they were all thinking. None of this would have happened if it wasn't for him. He felt sick.

'But we can't be lost,' Andy said. 'I mean, we haven't even come very far, have we?'

'That's just it,' Toby said. 'None of us knows. Does anyone even know what time Jay . . . I mean, what time we all left the course?'

Once again, nobody knew.

'We weren't supposed to cross that track,' Toby said. 'We shouldn't be here. These woods are big. At least six kilometres on each side. It would have been all right if we'd known which direction we were walking in, but we could have been walking around in circles. We probably have.'

Jay could hear the panic in Toby's voice, and he could see the others had noticed it too.

'But there must be *some* way we can find our way back,' Priya said shakily. 'Isn't there?'

There was a gloomy silence. Wind rustled in the brown leaves above their heads and they heard the long bubbling cry of a curlew on the moors in the distance. It seemed to grow a little darker beneath the trees.

Andy looked over Toby's shoulder at the map that was spread on the ground. 'Where is this wood we're in?' he asked.

Toby indicated a large patch of green with his finger. 'We're somewhere in this lot,' he said.

Andy looked at the map and frowned. 'Well, we want to get back onto the moors, don't we? I mean, we want to try and finish the course, even if we're a bit late. If we go east, then we'll probably hit the track, and even if we miss it, we can get back up high and we might be able to see where we are.'

Abby clapped Andy on the back. 'You're right,' she said. 'I knew you had some brains in there somewhere. Don't you see?' she said excitedly to the others. 'Say we're here' – she pointed at the map – 'then if we go east we'll hit the track eventually. The same if we're here. And if we're here' – she pointed to a spot further to the north – 'then we'll still come out on the moors, and at least we'll be able to see something.'

'That sounds good,' said Priya hesitantly. 'Can we do that, Connor?'

Connor stared at Toby's map. 'I don't know,' he said. 'It *sounds* OK. My dad's always telling me stories about getting lost. Grandpa too. There are things you're supposed to do. It's just, we have to be sure . . .'

Jay realized that everyone was waiting for Connor to decide. He could see how hard it was and he felt bad. He'd got them into this mess, and he suddenly wished that he knew how to help them get out of it.

'OK,' Connor said at last. 'It's too cold to sit around any longer. Priya, you're shivering. Are you OK?'

Priya nodded.

'Right, then,' he decided. 'Let's go.'

He set off with his compass in his hand; the others fell into line behind him, with Jay and Toby at the back.

'Can I see the map?' Jay asked Toby after a few minutes, when Connor stopped to check the direction they were heading.

Toby handed it to him.

'I didn't know this wood was so big,' Jay said. 'I never meant to run so far. I thought I could just hide for a bit and then go back to the car park.'

'Well,' replied Toby, 'it doesn't go on for ever. They're right. If we keep walking in this direction we'll come out sooner or later.'

'I suppose so,' said Jay. 'I'm sorry, Toby.'

'OK,' replied Toby. 'But listen. I've got a feeling we're going to need your navigation skills before this is over. You will help, won't you?'

'I'll try,' replied Jay. He found it hard to believe that any of them would want help from him.

They continued walking. After a few minutes

the trees began to thin out a little and there were patches of grass and brambles in between them.

'Hey, look!' said Abby suddenly. 'Isn't that a path?'

Connor stopped. She was pointing off to the left. 'Go and look, Abby,' he said as Andy took his camcorder out of the top of his rucksack and filmed her struggling through the tangled undergrowth.

'It is!' she called, and Jay felt a weight lift from his shoulders. If there was a path, then it must go *somewhere*, and this path was going in exactly the right direction. Nothing could change what had already happened, but if they got back quickly, it wouldn't seem quite so bad.

They all made their way over to join Abby. The path was narrow but it was definitely heading east across gently rising ground. Looking ahead, Jay could see some bigger gaps appearing between the trees.

'This looks right,' Connor said. 'Well done, Abby. I would never have spotted it.'

'It's not a very big path,' Toby said doubtfully.

'I know,' said Connor. 'But it goes in the right direction, that's the main thing. And we can get along much quicker now we don't have to struggle over all that rough ground.'

'The trees are thinner up ahead,' Andy put in. 'I'm sure they are. I bet we'll be back in no time. I'm going to run up there and film you all coming up the track.'

He raced ahead. Connor laughed and quickly set off after him. Abby and Priya came next, chatting excitedly in their relief at not being lost any more. Toby and Jay followed on behind.

We can do it, thought Jay. *We can still finish the course.*

Connor set a fast pace along the path, and soon they were all breathing hard. After a few minutes the trees seemed to press more closely on either side of them and they found themselves going uphill. There was no sign of the wood coming to an end, and the path narrowed, so that each of them had to push aside branches that reached across in front of them, and then hold them back to stop them snapping across the face of the person behind.

'I don't like this,' said Priya as a bramble snagged her trousers and the thorns bit into her leg. 'It doesn't look as if anyone ever comes along here.'

There was a sudden movement in the trees to their left, and something came crashing through the undergrowth towards them. Connor's heart thumped in his chest. Priya screamed, and right ahead of them a deer burst out of the wood and bounded off along the path. Connor stared after it. He took a few more steps and looked down at the fresh tracks in the mud, each print a pair of ovals, side by side. He'd noticed other prints on the path, but he'd paid no attention to them. He couldn't believe he'd been so stupid.

'It's a deer path, isn't it?' asked Toby as he drew alongside Connor.

Connor nodded.

'What does that mean?' Abby asked.

'It means it wasn't made by people at all,' Toby said. 'It means it might just go straight up onto the wildest parts of the moors, or into a bog, or anywhere. But one thing's for sure. It won't go where there are people.'

'So, what do we do now?' asked Andy. 'We've been walking for ages. We *must* be nearly out of these woods.'

'Maybe not,' said Toby, who was standing with his compass in his hand. 'This path has changed direction. I don't think we've been walking east at all. I think we've been heading north.'

Connor stared at him. He knew he'd made another foolish mistake. As soon as they reached the path he'd put his compass in his pocket and hadn't looked at it since. He fought down the feeling of panic that was rising up inside him. What if they couldn't find their way back? What if Rick had to call out the police and the mountain rescue people?

'Connor?' Priya said. 'What are we going to do?' Her eyes were wide with fear.

Connor realized that they were all looking at him, waiting for him to decide. 'We have to think this through properly,' he said. 'What do you think, Toby? What should we do now?'

Toby had the map in his hands. 'If the path keeps heading north,' he said slowly, 'then it will bring us out onto the moors up here somewhere. It goes quite high, but we should be able to see where we are. Only . . .'

'What?' asked Andy.

'We'll be a long way from where we started,' Toby went on. 'Really, we'll be heading in the wrong direction.'

'But we can't get through the woods here,' Abby said. 'The undergrowth's too thick. It would take for ever.'

'Connor?' said Jay. 'I've got an idea . . . Is that OK?'

Connor looked at him, surprised.

'We could go back,' Jay said, looking round at

the others. 'I know it seems stupid, but we could follow this path until we get to the place where we joined it. And then we could carry on eastwards again. It would be safer.'

Connor thought for a moment. Suddenly he heard his grandpa's voice inside his head. *Never be afraid to turn back, Connor. A lot of people get into difficulties because that's the one thing they don't consider. They think turning back is like admitting defeat, but sometimes it's the only sensible thing to do.*

'OK,' said Connor. 'I think that's what we should do.' He glanced at Jay and nodded his thanks.

The others groaned, but Connor picked up his rucksack and started to walk. There was another thing his grandpa always said: *First impressions aren't always right, Connor. When you get in a tricky situation, the most unexpected people sometimes come into their own.* Maybe, he thought, he'd got Jay wrong after all.

'You can see our footprints,' he said to the

others, looking at the marks in the muddy ground. 'We'll have to watch carefully to see where they stop. Everyone keep your eyes open.'

They set off wearily back down the path. 'This looks right,' said Priya after a while, when the trees began to thin and the path levelled out.

'It must be somewhere down here,' Abby said.

'Yes,' agreed Toby. 'But the ground's all rocky. There isn't a single footprint.'

'There has to be one somewhere,' Connor said. 'Maybe we left tracks when we came onto the path.'

'Hey, Andy,' said Abby. 'Don't do that now. We need everyone to look.'

Andy had stopped and was fiddling with his camcorder. He let out an excited yell. 'Look, everyone. I was filming – remember? See there. There's a big oak tree and a rowan beside it. It's the same place – look. I must have been standing right here!'

They all looked at the picture on the little screen. 'That's brilliant, Andy,' said Toby. 'I knew that camera had to be useful for something.'

'You can laugh,' said Andy with a grin. 'But this is going to be a really important movie when I've finished it. It'll show everyone all the things *not* to do when they go orienteering.'

Connor couldn't help smiling. Somehow, Andy always managed to stay cheerful. 'Yeah, well,' he said. 'It would be good if it also showed everyone how to get out of trouble. We'll start again from just over there, and this time I'm not following any paths that don't have tarmac on them and signposts saying where they go.'

CHAPTER 12

Connor led the way through the wood with his compass in his hand. Jay could see that he was finding it hard to steer a straight course. As they went on, the trees grew closer together and the undergrowth snatched at their legs. Jay had been surprised when Connor actually listened to his idea. And he couldn't help feeling pleased too. But it didn't seem to have helped them much. This was like walking through jungle. They needed machetes to hack their way through.

'This is nothing like the part of the wood we came through at first, is it?' asked Priya in a worried voice.

'Definitely not,' said Abby. A springy branch whipped across her face. 'Ouch!' she yelped. 'That hurt. Watch what you're doing, Andy.'

'Sorry,' said Andy. 'I couldn't stop it. Are you OK?'

'Yes, no thanks to you,' said Abby, checking with her hand to see if the branch had drawn blood.

'If it gets any thicker, we'll have to turn back,' Andy said. 'Whose stupid idea was this?'

Connor had been pressing on relentlessly through the dense undergrowth, but now he stopped and looked back.

'Where are we going?' Priya said, her voice rising. 'We're still lost, aren't we? We'll never find our way out of this.'

'Priya, stop,' said Abby anxiously. 'It's OK. Connor knows what he's doing.'

'But it's cold.' Priya shivered, her voice quiet again.

As soon as she said it, Jay became aware of the chilly breeze that was sneaking through the trees. He'd been walking fast, but now that he'd stopped, the sweat felt icy on his skin.

'We should put more clothes on,' Connor told them. 'Hats and gloves too.'

'I didn't bring any gloves,' Priya said miserably. 'I mean, it was sunny, and I thought we'd be finished by now.'

'It's OK,' said Toby, digging in his rucksack. 'I've got a spare pair. Here.'

'Nice one, Toby,' Abby said as Priya pulled on the gloves. She bundled her untidy hair into a woolly hat. 'You haven't got a flask of soup in there, have you?'

'Well, actually,' replied Toby, taking a small flask out of his rucksack, 'I've got some hot black-currant drink. Here, Priya – you have some first.'

He poured a little into a cup, and handed it to her. She took a sip and then passed the cup on to the others.

'Thanks, Toby,' said Connor. 'We'd better stop here and have something to eat. It's nearly half past one.'

They all took an assortment of sandwiches, chocolate bars and fruit out of their rucksacks.

Jay couldn't believe that it was a few hours since he'd been in the kitchen, watching his mum make his lunch. It seemed more like years. But sitting down to eat together almost made everything seem normal, especially when they washed down the sandwiches with sips of hot blackcurrant.

'It can't be much further now,' said Andy. 'We'll probably walk out of these woods and find ourselves on that track.'

'Right,' said Abby, smiling round at the others as she tucked some escaping hair back into her hat. 'I bet we'll be back at the minibus and laughing about all this in an hour or so.'

Abby was amazing, thought Jay. It seemed as if there was nothing that could ever get her down. He didn't think anyone was going to be laughing when they turned up at the car park. It was obvious now that even if they did find their way back, they'd never complete the course in time. Connor shook his head, and Jay could see that he was thinking the same thing.

'Connor?' said Priya. 'What about the phone? Can't you call Rick and tell him what's happened? Someone might already have noticed that we've not been to any other control points. What if they've already told our parents they don't know where we are?'

'Priya's right,' said Toby, and Connor started to reach into his rucksack for the phone.

'No,' said Abby. 'Don't do it yet, Connor. I'm sure they won't start to worry until two o'clock. As long as we're back on the course by then it'll be OK. We can still make it, can't we?'

Connor thought back over all the wrong decisions he'd made today – he knew he'd got it wrong from the start. The moment Jay had run off he should have got the phone out and called Rick. Suddenly it all seemed obvious to him. The only reason he hadn't called in was because he knew he'd been completely, totally wrong to yell at Jay. He'd let them all down and he was just going to have to admit it. He suddenly remembered that his grandparents were driving up to watch them finish. 'Sorry, Abby,' he said. 'We really do have to call.'

He took out the phone and switched it on with trembling fingers. It was for emergencies only, and just holding it in his hands made him realize that this really *was* an emergency. He found Rick's name and pressed the dial button. The phone beeped at him. He stared disbelievingly at the display. 'There's no signal,' he told the others. 'None at all.'

'There must be,' said Priya. 'Give it to me.' She grabbed the phone from Connor and punched frantically at the buttons, struggling to hold back the tears.

Abby took it gently out of her hands. 'It's OK, Priya,' she said in a slightly shaky voice. 'Don't cry. We're bound to get a signal soon. And with any luck we won't even need to call. Not if we get to a checkpoint.'

'Abby's right,' said Connor. 'Let's move. Honestly, Priya, it'll be all right.'

They all fastened up their rucksacks. Abby took a last bite of her apple and dropped the core on the ground. She saw Toby's green eyes watching at her. 'What?' she asked. 'It'll rot, won't it?'

Toby bent down and picked up the apple core. He popped it into a plastic bag in the side pocket of his rucksack. 'I don't like leaving anything behind,' he said. 'Come on, let's go.'

The Tigers pressed on through the woods. Gradually the trees began to thin and they were climbing more steeply. Now there was heather underfoot again, and solid rock. The wind suddenly grew stronger and began to catch at their clothes.

'What do we do now?' asked Priya. Her face was still pale and streaked with tears.

Connor paused. 'Have you got your Ordnance Survey map, Toby?' he asked.

Toby put the map on the ground and they all looked at it as he pointed. 'I think we're at the edge of the woods now,' he said, looking around.

There were still occasional trees dotted about, but ahead of them there was only grass and heather. 'What do you think, Jay?'

'Go on,' Connor urged Jay. 'Have a look.' He could see that Jay was still feeling awkward, but he knew that Toby reckoned Jay was very good at navigation. Maybe he really could help.

Jay leaned over the map. 'The track's never more than a few hundred metres from the edge of the wood,' he said. 'So, if we carry on due east for, say, four hundred metres, then we'll either find it, or we'll know we're too far north.'

'Well, this definitely isn't where we were earlier,' Connor said. 'There's no sign of any marshy stuff.' He thought for a moment. 'We'll do what Jay says and go straight on. Four hundred metres ought to take us about six minutes on the flat, but we're going uphill and it's quite rough. I reckon we should walk for about fifteen minutes. OK?'

They all nodded their agreement.

Connor looked up at the rise ahead of him. 'I

bet when we get to the top of this bit we'll be able to see where we are,' he said. 'The track might even be right there, just on the other side.'

He tried to make his voice sound more confident than he felt. There was something about this wild, lonely hillside that was different from the part of the moors where they'd been earlier. In his heart, he didn't really believe they would find the track so easily. But maybe, he told himself, it just looked different when the sun was shining. He checked the bearing and headed on up the hill.

They soon left the last of the trees behind and climbed upwards over lumpy, uneven ground. Connor tried to keep up a steady pace, and glanced at his watch frequently. The minutes ticked by and there was still no sign of the track.

'We're aiming for that rock on the skyline,' he told the others, pointing ahead to where a shape stood up like a pillar against the grey sky. 'When we get there, we should be able to see.'

'Great!' said Andy, striding past Connor and

racing on up the hill. 'I'll get there first and shoot some footage of you lot coming up.'

'Be careful,' Connor called after him. 'You could fall and break something.'

'Not me,' yelled Andy. 'I'm like a mountain goat. Abby's the one who has accidents.'

With that, his foot caught on a heather root and he went flying, head over heels.

'Andy!' Connor yelled. 'Are you all right? Andy!'

There was no reply. He climbed quickly up to where Andy had disappeared and found him lying on his back in the heather.

'Sorry,' gasped Andy. 'I can't . . . get my breath.'

'Honestly!' said Connor. He reached out a hand and pulled Andy to his feet as the others joined them. 'Are you OK?'

'Sure,' Andy replied. 'I came down flat on my back. It knocked all the breath out of me, that's all.'

'And look,' said Abby crossly. 'Look at that rock. What if your head had hit that?'

'Well, it didn't, did it?' Andy rubbed his head.

'And we're nearly at the top. You lot go on and I'll film you from here.'

Connor was about to tell him how stupid he'd been, but as he opened his mouth to speak he saw Andy look down at the rock. It was very close to where his head had been, and help was a long way away. Andy's face went very pale, and Connor knew that there was no need to say anything more.

Andy took the camcorder from the top of his rucksack and checked it over. 'It's OK,' he said unsteadily. 'Go on, then. You'll look good against that sky. It's like that movie we watched at school – *Wuthering Heights*.'

They climbed up to the pillar of rock and stopped. What lay ahead of them scared Connor, and he could see the shock on the faces of the others. There was no sign of a track. Instead they saw open moorland that disappeared into grey mist. Even as they watched, more mist spread across the hillside. The air was cold and wet in their faces.

'It's not mist,' said Toby suddenly. 'Those are clouds. We should get our waterproofs on right now or we're going to get soaked.'

At least we got that right, thought Connor grimly as they pulled waterproof jackets and trousers out of their rucksacks. He was glad he had checked everyone's kit carefully before they'd started.

'Just in time,' said Abby as a finger of cloud swirled around them and fine rain pattered on their hoods. 'But what now? We're even more lost than we were before.'

'I don't like this, Connor,' said Priya. 'I don't like this at all.'

Connor looked over at her. He could tell that she was really frightened. For a moment he felt panic rising up inside him again – but then he realized that they were all waiting for him. Even Toby. It was his job to keep them all going, to get them home safely. He felt a familiar shape in his pocket – his grandpa's knife. And suddenly he heard his grandpa's voice again: *We're not lost,*

Connor, we're just temporarily not quite sure exactly where we are. We'll have a think, then we'll carry on and see if we can collect some more information.

'Toby,' he said. 'Have you got your map?'

Toby took it out, and rain spattered on the plastic bag. Connor wiped it away. 'We're somewhere on this part of the moor,' Toby said, pointing. Then he paused. 'I'm an idiot!' he exclaimed. 'I bought this expensive altimeter watch and I haven't even used it. He pressed a button on his watch. 'There! We're at five hundred metres. On this contour here . . .' He pointed to a line on the map.

'Right,' agreed Jay. 'But the trouble is, we don't know exactly where on that line we are.'

'We can find out,' Toby said. 'If we keep walking east, staying at the same height, we'll hit one of these streams and then we'll know. They both go down off the moor to the south, see? We could follow either of them and we'd get back to safety eventually. Look – this first one goes down right behind the car park.'

They all looked to the east, where the bleak moorland vanished into mist and cloud. 'We can't go that way,' cried Priya. 'Connor, we can't. We won't be able to see. We—'

'It's OK, Priya,' Abby said firmly. 'We've been in the mountains in weather like this before. Right, Andy?'

Andy nodded. 'I know it looks bad,' he said, 'but it was just like this last summer in Wales.'

'I think we have to go on,' decided Connor, looking gratefully at Abby and Andy. He could tell that they were just as worried as he was, but they were doing their best to keep Priya's spirits up. 'We can't go back,' he explained to her now. 'There was no phone signal down there, and there's none here either. We need to let someone know where we are as soon as we can. Do you think you can make it?'

Priya sniffed and nodded. They all stood there for a moment as the mist and rain drifted across the desolate landscape. It seemed mad to go on into those clouds, but Connor knew it was the right thing to do.

'There's no sense waiting,' he said. 'If we walk due east and stay at the same height, we can't help but find one of those streams. Just make sure that you all stay close and no one lags behind. Can we have a guess at how long it ought to take, Toby?'

Toby and Jay both looked at the map. 'We're somewhere along here,' Jay said.

'It'll be at least eight hundred metres before we find either stream,' said Toby, 'which is . . .'

'Twelve minutes at four kph,' Jay said quickly. 'But the ground's very rough and the visibility is terrible. We should walk for at least double that. Twenty-four minutes.'

Connor thought Jay might get angry when he'd mentioned lagging behind, but he hadn't. It was almost as if, the worse things got, the more Jay was enjoying himself. He was surprisingly tough, and he seemed to be just as good at maths as Toby. Suddenly, unexpectedly, Connor felt glad that Jay was with them. He heaved his rucksack onto his back. 'Right, then,' he said. 'Maybe we should all count our steps too.'

It was a pity, he thought, that they hadn't been this careful right from the start.

Tiger Patrol fell into line, and their hooded shapes melted quickly into the mist.

CHAPTER 13

'That's it, then,' said Connor. 'Twenty-two minutes.'

'I've been counting steps,' Abby said. 'I only make it seven hundred metres.'

'How about the rest of you?' asked Connor.

'I make it the same as Abby,' Andy told him. 'More or less.'

'Me too,' said Toby and Jay together.

'This is a horrible place . . .' Priya shivered.

They stood together in a little semicircle with their backs to the wind and the rain. Jay felt a knot of anxiety in his stomach. This had been his idea, even if Connor had taken the final decision. When he'd been looking at the map, he'd been thinking about what to do as if it was a problem in a computer game. But in a computer game, if you went wrong you could just start again as many times as you liked, even if you'd been blown up by a photon torpedo . . . This was real. What if they couldn't find the stream?

'It's OK,' said Toby. 'I know it feels scary, but we're doing the right things. We all looked at the map. And my watch says we're still at an altitude of five hundred metres. We might find the stream any time now. Counting steps isn't that accurate on rough ground like this. It's only an estimate.'

'You're right,' Connor said. 'We must be quite close. All we have to do is keep walking in this direction.'

'You know what?' said Jay. Connor's words had made him feel more confident. 'This is actually exactly like Level Eight of *Galactic Explorer*. When you get down onto the surface of the gas giant planet and you're out there in your space-suit, you can't see a thing. You have to steer blind, just using the on-screen map and the radar and the ultrasound. Only there are aliens trying to shoot you up too.'

'At least there are no aliens here,' replied Toby light-heartedly.

'Oh, I don't know,' said Andy. 'What's that over there?'

Priya screamed as something big and dark loomed up at them through the mist. It appeared to change shape – and it was growing. Priya grabbed Abby's arm.

'It's a hill,' said Toby uncertainly. 'Forget about aliens. Only . . . there shouldn't be any hills over there.'

'It's OK,' called Connor from up ahead. 'It's just a rock. Look – it must be some kind of optical illusion. And listen! Can you hear what I can hear?'

They stood in silence for a moment. Somewhere to their right there was a tinkling, gurgling sound. 'It's water!' yelled Abby. 'We've found it! Hey, Connor, that's awesome! Brilliant, Jay! Come on, everyone, let's go and see.'

'Wait,' said Connor, but there was no stopping her. Just as she was about to vanish into the mist, they all heard a piercing shriek and Abby stopped dead.

'Sorry,' said Toby, taking a whistle from his lips. 'I had to stop you, Abby. We must all stay together.'

'OK, OK,' said Abby. 'I wouldn't have got lost, though. Look. The stream's right here.'

'Thanks, Toby,' Connor said. 'That could have been a disaster. Hang on – I'm going to check the phone. It won't be quite so bad ringing up now we know roughly where we are.' He looked at the screen. 'I don't believe it,' he said, shaking his head. 'There's still no signal.'

'But everything's OK now, isn't it?' Priya said happily. 'All we have to do is follow the stream and it'll take us back. We're safe.'

'It's not quite that simple,' said Jay, who had been working things out in his head. 'We walked for nearly forty minutes in the end. I think we might have missed the first stream. Let's have a look at your map, Toby.'

He took the map and lined it up with the

compass so that everything was facing in the right direction. 'Both of the streams start off in the same direction,' he said. 'But it would be better to follow the first one if we can.'

'I bet this *is* the first one,' Andy said. 'We just walked more slowly than we thought, that's all. And besides, how could we have missed a stream?'

'Well, look at it,' Connor said. 'It's not very big, is it? The first one might have been even smaller. I don't know about you lot, but I was expecting something like the one down in the car park, but of course they're really small up here. We could have walked right over it without noticing.'

'And if this *is* the second one,' Jay pointed out, 'then even when we get down off the moor we'll still have a long way to walk.'

'We should go back,' Toby said gloomily. 'We should go a hundred metres south from here and then walk back west again for about five hundred metres. If we haven't found a stream by then, we'll know that this is the right one.'

'I don't want to go back,' said Priya in a small voice. 'Please, Connor – we don't have to, do we?'

'We can just follow this stream down,' said Andy. 'Once we're off the moor and out of this weather, then we'll be safe. That's the most important thing, isn't it?'

Toby looked at the map doubtfully. 'If this is the *second* stream,' he said, 'then it gets bigger quite fast. There's lots of other streams that join it – look. Lots of little side valleys. It might not be that simple to follow it.'

'If it's bigger, then it ought to be easier to follow,' said Abby, putting an arm around Priya. 'Both the streams go down off this moor, and that's all I care about, OK? I'm sick of stumbling about in this mist, and so is Priya. What about you, Andy?'

'I don't know,' Andy said. 'It seems like a good idea to get down as fast as we can, but—'

'There you are,' Abby said to Connor. 'Three of us want to go down this way.'

Jay waited. Connor's decision wasn't easy, and Jay was glad that *he* didn't have to make it.

'I think we have to go down now,' Connor said finally. 'It's nearly three o'clock already. What matters most is letting Rick know we're OK. It might take us half an hour to find that other stream, and if we don't, then we'll have to come back here anyway. So we'll follow this one. OK, everyone?'

Priya nodded happily. Toby was silent for a second, then said, 'You're right, Connor. We have to report in as soon as we can.'

'How about you, Jay?' asked Connor. 'What do you think?'

Connor's question caught Jay by surprise. 'I . . . I think you're right,' he said.

'OK.' Connor gave Jay a quick smile. 'Let's go.'

Connor led the way. It soon became obvious that this *was* the second of the two streams. After a couple of hundred metres a second trickle joined it from the right, and then two bigger streams came in from the left, and suddenly their stream looked more like a small river, tumbling over rocks in a small valley of its own that was bordered on either side by low cliffs.

'I can't see the moors any more,' said Priya.

'Great!' said Abby. 'I don't care if I never see them again. And I'm sure it looks brighter down there. It's stopped raining too.'

'I don't suppose . . .' began Priya.

'What?' asked Abby.

'Well, I was just wondering. Do you think there's any chance we could still get our badges? It would be my first one.'

Abby shook her head. 'You ought to get one for being brave,' she said. 'I don't suppose I'd have done as well as you if this had happened on my first expedition. But we'll never have time to finish the course. I shouldn't think there's the tiniest chance we'll get badges.'

'Me neither,' agreed Toby.

'Hey, listen,' said Andy. 'I think I can hear a waterfall!'

The banks of the stream were smooth and grassy, and they all ran forward towards the sound.

'Wait!' called Connor, who had paused to check the phone again, with no result. 'Be careful!'

They all stopped – just in time. The little valley they had been following came to a sudden end as the stream rushed over a cliff and crashed into a deep pool about fifteen metres below them.

'Rats,' said Toby. 'Now we'll *have* to go back.'

'But this is amazing,' said Andy. 'I never knew there were places like this up here. I'm going up to get some shots of all of you and the waterfall.' He pointed to a rocky ledge away to their right that followed the side of the valley for a little way and ended in a platform overlooking the waterfall.

'I don't think you should,' said Connor. 'It's very narrow.'

'I'll be fine,' Andy said. 'I'll stop if it looks dangerous.'

'I'm going to explore too,' said Abby. 'I'm not letting Andy have all the fun.'

Connor couldn't believe it. Just because they weren't totally lost any more they seemed to think everything was fine. But it wasn't. They were going to have to retrace their steps again and lose even more time . . .

'Can't we take a break?' Jay said unexpectedly. 'Priya looks really tired.'

Connor looked at the others. Jay was right. They'd had a bad time on the moor, and if they were an extra few minutes late it wasn't going to make any difference now. 'OK,' he said – and saw Priya look gratefully at Jay. 'We'll stop for five minutes, but then we'll have to go back and look for a way out of this valley. We should all have something to eat and drink. Would anyone like some of my grandpa's cake?'

He unwrapped the second package and carved off lumps with his knife, handing them round to the others. They were all still chewing when they heard Andy's voice.

'Hey, you lot!' he called. They looked up and saw him perched high on the valley wall, aiming his camcorder at them. 'That's really cool,' he said. 'It looks like you're on a proper adventure. Discovering a lost world or something.'

'Can we get out of the valley that way?' yelled Toby.

Andy peered upwards. Small trees and ferns clung to the cliff face above him, and it didn't look so very far to the top, but he shook his head. 'I don't think so,' he replied. 'It's just rock, going straight up.' Then he looked down to where the stream plunged over the edge. 'This waterfall is brilliant, though. Maybe there's a cave behind it, like in a book I read. I . . .' He paused.

Connor heard something in his voice. 'What is it?' he asked. 'What can you see?'

'I'm not sure . . .' Andy replied. 'I just thought – maybe there's a route down beside the waterfall.'

'No way,' said Connor. 'We're not going down there, Andy. It's too dangerous.'

'Sure . . . But – you know what? I'm pretty certain there's a path coming up the valley further down there. If we could just somehow get to the bottom, then we'd be safe.'

'Well, we're not doing it,' said Connor, aware that the others were watching him. 'Did anyone notice how far back it was that the sides of the valley became cliffs?'

'Not that far,' Toby said. He was looking at his map. 'It's just really annoying to have to turn back again, that's all.'

'What, so you want to climb down?' Connor suddenly felt exhausted.

'No,' said Toby. 'I'm just fed up. We all are.'

'We shouldn't have come right down beside the river,' Priya said. 'My brother told me it could be dangerous. We should have stayed up high and just kept it in sight.'

'Well, why didn't you say that before?' Connor asked her. 'It's not much use now, is it?'

Priya's face fell, and instantly he felt ashamed. What made it worse was that as soon as Priya had said it, he remembered his dad telling him exactly the same thing. 'I'm sorry,' he said to her. 'It's not your fault. I should have known myself.'

'It doesn't matter whose fault it is,' said Jay. 'We'll get back OK now, won't we? It's just going to take a bit longer, that's all. We're not lost any more.'

'Jay's right,' said Toby.

Connor rubbed his eyes and tried to concentrate, but it was no good. He could only think of one thing. 'We should have finished the course ages ago. They'll have started looking for us already, I should think. And this stupid phone's useless.'

'That's not your fault either,' Jay said. He paused for a moment and took a deep breath. 'None of this is your fault, Connor. No one can blame you. And I'll tell them that. I don't care what they think. They'll never let me stay in the Scouts anyway.'

'No!' said Priya. 'They can't make you leave . . . Can they?'

'Of course they won't,' said Toby. 'Don't worry, Jay. Everybody's allowed to make mistakes. It's what you do afterwards that matters. Right, Connor?'

But Connor was staring towards the waterfall, a horrified look on his face. 'Where's Abby?' he asked.

Right at that moment they heard a shout from Andy. 'Connor!' he yelled. 'Toby! Come quick!' He was pointing at something down beside the waterfall.

They ran forward, and Connor peered over the edge of the cliff. He saw Abby's face staring up at him, very white and scared. She was about halfway down, clinging to the wet rock with her fingertips while her feet rested on a narrow ledge. Spray from the waterfall blew across her face.

'I can't move,' she said. Her voice was almost a whisper. 'Help me, please. I think I'm going to fall.'

CHAPTER 14

Connor didn't hesitate. He could see that Abby was close to panicking. 'I'll have to climb down,' he said. 'Where did you start, Abby?'

'There's . . . there's a little tree . . .' She took one hand off the rock to point, and for a terrible moment they all thought she was going to fall. She seemed to be teetering on the ledge, and her hand flailed in the air, then scrabbled at the rock. Small stones went flying down the cliff, and then her fingers found a grip and she pressed herself flat against the face of the cliff. Her shoulders were shaking.

'Don't move,' Connor said, his heart beating fast. 'I can find a way down. Just hold on, Abby. I'll be there as soon as I can.'

'You can't!' said Priya. 'Connor, you can't go

down there. What if you fall? What if both of you fall?' She started to cry.

Connor turned and saw fear in Jay's eyes too. Toby had turned away and was frantically emptying his rucksack.

'There's no other way,' he said. 'I know what I'm doing, Priya. If Abby climbed down, then I can too, OK?'

Jay saw Priya bite her lip and nod as Connor began to search for a good place to start climbing. He felt strange – kind of dizzy and light-headed – and scared. One brief glimpse over the edge had been enough. He'd seen the terrified look on Abby's face.

Andy scrambled down from the ledge where he'd been filming. His face was pale. 'How did it happen?' Jay asked him.

'I could see a way down,' Andy said quietly. 'You know what Abby's like – she just went for it. She said she could climb down. I think she must have gone wrong.'

'Why didn't you stop her?'

'Are you kidding? I was right up there' – he pointed – 'I couldn't exactly grab her arm, could I?'

'You could have called us.'

Andy looked at the ground. 'I know. I should have done. But I thought she could do it. There really *is* a way down, you know.'

'OK,' Connor called down to Abby. 'I'm starting now. Do you think, if I help you, you can climb back up again?'

'I . . . I don't know. I'll try.'

Connor turned to Andy. 'Can you keep talking to her?' he asked. 'That way I can concentrate on climbing down.'

Andy gulped and nodded. 'I'm sorry, Connor. I should have told you what she was doing. I thought it would be a good surprise.'

'It was a surprise, all right,' said Connor grimly. 'Right, here goes.'

'Wait,' called Toby anxiously.

Jay looked round and saw that Toby had taken

everything out of his rucksack. There was an enormous pile, all neatly packed in different-coloured bags.

'I know I put it in,' Toby said. 'I saw it in the cupboard and thought it was just possible we might need it, and now . . . Yes! Here it is!' He pulled a coil of rope from the very bottom of his rucksack and held it up triumphantly.

Connor looked at the rope. 'Do you think it's long enough?' he said.

Toby stepped forward and paid it out carefully down the cliff. The end dangled beside Abby's head. His face fell. 'Too short,' he said. 'Much too short once we've put a loop in it. Sorry, Connor.'

'Well, it's pretty amazing that you thought of bringing it in the first place,' Connor replied. 'But I'll just have to go down without it. We can't wait any longer.'

Jay took a couple of steps forward and looked down at the cliff face. He saw Abby clinging to the rock and suddenly felt dizzy again as he looked past her to the jumble of rocks below and the dark pool at the foot of the waterfall. If she fell . . .

He took a deep breath. He had an idea and he needed to study the cliff carefully. It wasn't completely smooth. Most of the way down he could see that there were ledges and cracks, and in places bushes and small trees were growing. The sound of the waterfall was loud in his ears.

'Jay,' said Connor. 'What are you doing? Get back from there.'

'It's OK,' he replied. 'I think we could do it in stages. You see that little tree right above where Abby is? We can rope you up and you can climb down to there. At least . . . I mean, it looks really hard. I don't know how good you are at climbing. Could you do it?'

Connor came over to stand beside Jay and looked over. 'I think so,' he said. 'There's even a proper ledge to stand on once I'm there.'

'Then someone else can climb down too, and they can hold the rope while you go down to Abby,' Jay continued. 'That way you'll be protected all the time. It'll be much safer.'

Connor, Toby and Andy all stared at Jay. He felt himself flushing. 'It's only an idea,' he said. 'I mean, I don't suppose it'll work. I know I couldn't climb down there myself.'

'Of course it'll work,' said Toby. 'Connor can climb anything. That's brilliant, Jay.' He picked up the rope. 'Here, Connor – I'll tie it round your waist.' He started muttering under his breath: 'Make the rabbit hole. Up comes the rabbit' – he pulled the end of the rope up through the loop he'd made – 'round the tree, and back down the hole.' Finally he pulled the knot tight.

'Are you sure that's the right knot?' asked Priya anxiously.

'It's a bowline. It's good as long as there's a load on it. You should keep checking it, Connor.'

Connor nodded. 'Who's going to come down after me?'

'Have either of you done much climbing?' Toby asked Jay and Priya.

Jay shook his head. He'd never climbed anything.

'I couldn't,' whispered Priya.

'What about you, Andy?' said Toby. 'You're much better at climbing than I am.'

As soon as Toby spoke, Jay realized that Andy had been talking quietly the whole time. He was lying on the grass with his face way out over the edge so that Abby could hear him. 'Remember last summer at camp,' he was saying now. 'When Sajiv thought there was a dead cow in the field and he wanted to tell the farmer – but it was only asleep?'

'Don't!' Abby's voice floated up from below, almost drowned by the sound of rushing water. She was half laughing, half crying. 'I mustn't laugh. I'll fall.'

'It had better be you, Toby,' Connor said quietly. 'Let Andy carry on with what he's doing.'

Toby nodded. Jay could see how nervous he was. 'You and Priya will have to hold the rope,' Toby said to Jay. 'I'll put it round this tree first and you can let it out a bit at a time.'

Jay took hold of the rope. Priya grabbed the end behind him, and he could feel her trembling. 'It's going to be OK,' he told her as Connor's head disappeared over the edge of the cliff, watched anxiously by Toby and Andy. 'Connor knows what he's doing.'

'I hope so,' said Priya.

Connor's pulse was racing as he lowered himself over the cliff-edge. It was one thing climbing on crags in Wales in a hard hat and a harness, but this was something else entirely. He glanced anxiously at Toby's knot, but it seemed solid enough. Trust Toby to bring a rope – *and* to know the right knot to use. He thought how strange it was that a simple thing like a knot could actually save your life. Then his foot slipped and he banged his face against the rock as he fought frantically to regain his balance.

'Are you OK?' Toby called anxiously from above.

'Fine,' yelled Connor, waiting for his heartbeat to slow down. His hands were trembling. 'I'm going on now.'

The stinging pain reminded him to concentrate. Carefully he worked his way downwards. It was simple at first. There were good solid holds and it was more like a hard scramble than a climb. He could see why Abby had been tempted. Then he heard Toby's voice from above him:

'You need to move over to your left. Can you see the tree?'

Connor placed his feet firmly on a narrow ledge and leaned out as far as he dared, but he still couldn't see it. 'There's a sort of buttress,' he said. 'The cliff bulges out. I couldn't really see what it was like from where you are. I guess I'll have to climb over it.'

He moved out to his left, reaching with his foot for a projecting lump of rock. It was a very small lump, but his foot found it and it seemed solid enough. There was a good-looking hand-hold above. He transferred his weight onto his left foot, reached up, and grabbed onto it. He rested, breathing hard, and suddenly felt a cold sweat break out all over his body. Below him the rock fell away sheer. The cliff wasn't that high, but it felt as if there was a 300-metre drop below him. If he fell from here, he would have no chance. What if Priya and Jay let the rope slip? What if that tree wasn't strong enough?

He forced himself to take deep breaths. Then he heard Toby's voice again.

'Connor? Why have you stopped? What's up?'

'It's OK,' he said, trying to make his voice sound calm. 'I'm going on again now.'

He could see what he had to do. On the climbing wall at the sports centre in town it would have been an easy move. He'd done harder things hundreds of times, but suddenly his arms and legs didn't seem to be working.

'Connor?' Abby's voice sounded very small below him. 'My fingers are hurting. I don't know how long I can hold on.'

The fear in her voice cleared Connor's head. He closed his eyes and tried to imagine he was on the climbing wall, held safely in a harness. There was a red hold at about nine o'clock to his left. He had to lift his leg like so, and then push up, and . . .

He opened his eyes and grunted with the effort as he grabbed onto a ledge above his head. He stopped again for a moment and looked back at the bulging rock he had just come round. He'd climbed that! Just for a second a feeling of exhilaration washed over him. And then he looked down and saw Abby a few metres below. She was shivering, and as a gust of wind blew icy spray from the waterfall into his face he understood why. They had no time to waste.

'Not long now,' he called down to her. He took hold of the tree and gave it a good shake. The trunk wasn't much thicker than his wrist, but it seemed solidly anchored to the rock. He lifted the loop of rope over his head. 'Pull it up,' he called up to Jay. He could just see his head, peering over the edge. 'You can come down now, Toby. But listen – there must be a better way. I went down too far.'

At the top of the cliff Jay and Priya pulled the rope up. Priya coiled it tidily using her hand and her elbow before handing it to Toby.

'That's neat,' said Jay, watching how she did it.

Toby checked the knot and pulled the loop over his head. He looked nervously over the edge, and Jay knew exactly how he felt. It gave him the shivers every time he had to look down.

Toby paused. 'Hey, Andy,' he said. 'If you went back up to that ledge where you were filming, do you think you could see the best way down?'

'Well, yes,' replied Andy. 'But shouldn't I stay down here to help Abby?'

'Connor's close to her now,' Toby said. 'Go on. I . . . I'd feel much better.'

Andy set off up to his perch above the water-fall. Jay thought it looked nearly as dangerous as the cliff below them, but Andy made it back to the little platform safely. 'You were right, Toby,' he called back above the noise of the rushing water. 'You need to start a bit further to your right, nearer to the stream.'

Toby moved along a short distance until Andy called down: 'That's it. Right there.'

He looked doubtfully at the sheer drop below him.

'It's OK, honest,' Andy yelled. 'There's a ledge just below you that you can't see from where you are.'

Toby shot an anxious glance at Jay and Priya. 'Don't worry,' Priya told him. 'I feel much better now. And Jay's really strong. We won't let you fall.'

Toby smiled at her gratefully. Priya seemed to have recovered from her earlier panic and her face was full of determination. He got down on his hands and knees and worked his way cautiously backwards until his legs were hanging over the edge. Jay heard his feet scrabbling around briefly, and then he sighed with relief as he found solid rock.

'What did I tell you?' said Andy. 'You can climb straight down from there.'

Connor looked up and saw Toby coming carefully towards him. 'Not long now,' he called down to Abby, and a few moments later Toby was standing on the ledge beside him. Connor reached out and squeezed his shoulder.

Toby looked up. 'I've made it,' he yelled. 'Let the rope down.'

'OK,' came Jay's voice. 'Here it comes.'

The rope came slithering down the cliff. Connor quickly coiled it up and took a couple of turns around the small tree that was growing from the rock, then he handed the coils to Toby. 'I'll go down to Abby and get the rope on her. I'll let her climb up first, and then you can send it down for me, OK?'

Toby nodded, and Connor worked his way swiftly down to Abby. She was very close to the waterfall, and the spray battered him as he climbed. It was lucky they had waterproofs on, but even so, when he reached Abby he saw that she was shivering.

'You'll have to take your hands off the rock one at a time so I can get the rope round your waist,' he said. 'I'll put my arm around your back so you can't fall off, OK?'

Abby nodded. Connor slipped the loop over her head, then over her arms, one at a time, and checked that it was secure. 'There,' he said. 'Now you're safe. You can't fall. All you have to do is climb up. I'll show you where to put your feet and hands. Look – put your right foot here.' He pointed to a deep foot-hold about forty centimetres above Abby's right foot.

But Abby seemed to be frozen to the rock. Connor saw her move her foot a tiny fraction, but she instantly put it back. 'I'm sorry,' she stammered through chattering teeth. 'I can't move, Connor. I just can't.'

CHAPTER 15

'Don't worry,' said Connor. 'If you can't go up, then we'll just have to get you down. One thing's for sure – you can't stay here.'

He tried to make his voice sound cheerful, but inside he was seriously worried. Abby hadn't been stuck on the rock for long, but it was cold and wet. She was shivering and probably suffering from shock. He knew that there was a real danger she'd soon be suffering from exposure too. They simply had to get her down, and warm.

'Toby,' he called. 'Do you think you can climb down here? It's not hard. We're going to have to help Abby all the way to the bottom.'

To Connor's relief, Toby didn't argue or ask questions.

'Listen,' Connor said to Abby. 'I'm sorry, but I'd better slip the rope off you again.'

Abby let out a little wail.

'You'll be OK,' he told her. 'We have to check that the rope is long enough, and it'll just get in Toby's way if he climbs down with it. You can feel my hand on your back, can't you? I won't let you fall.'

Very quickly, Connor lifted the rope over Abby's head again. 'You can let go,' he called to Toby. He watched as the end fell past him. It easily reached to the foot of the cliff. 'Toby, there's a good ledge just beside us,' he said. 'If you can get down there we'll be OK.'

'I'm going to help Connor,' Toby called up to Jay and Priya.

'Are you sure?' said Jay, poking his head over the edge of the cliff once more. 'You'll have to do it without a rope.'

'Connor says it's simple,' replied Toby, raising his voice to make himself heard over the roar of the waterfall. 'I'll be fine.'

Connor smiled to himself. He could hear that Jay was worried, and he knew that Priya must be too, but Toby was making a great job of reassuring them. And he knew Toby could do the climb. Toby always climbed slowly, and people often thought that was because he was scared, but Connor knew that he was simply being cautious – the way he was about everything, in fact.

Slowly and steadily Toby worked his way down to Connor and Abby, and knelt beside them on the ledge. He took the loop of rope from Connor's outstretched hand, then hauled the rest of it back up the cliff. He took a couple of turns around a large piece of rock before handing the loop back to Connor, who replaced it around Abby's waist.

'Are you ready?' Connor asked her.

'I don't think I can,' she said.

'You have to,' replied Connor firmly as he felt Toby take up the slack in the rope. 'I'll be holding onto you the whole way.'

Connor looked up at Andy, perched on his

ledge above the waterfall. 'Can you see the best way down?' he yelled.

Andy cupped his hands to his mouth. 'Away from the water,' he shouted. 'Down and to your right. There's something that looks almost like a path. It starts about three metres below you.'

'Right,' Connor said to Abby. 'I'm going to take your right foot and move it down about ten centimetres. Toby's got you on the rope. Can you feel?'

She gave the slightest of nods. Connor removed his hand from her back; she stiffened and clutched the rock even harder, but he quickly climbed down and found a solid position below her. He put his hand on Abby's foot. 'Take deep breaths,' he said, remembering how he'd felt climbing around the buttress. 'That's good. Now let me move your foot. Just stretch your leg down.'

The move only took a split second, but it seemed to last for ever.

'That's it!' said Connor. 'Doesn't that feel better?'

Abby nodded again.

'OK,' he went on. 'Now you need to bring the other foot down beside it. Keep your hands where they are.'

Slowly, very slowly, Connor and Toby helped Abby to climb down the cliff.

Up above, Priya and Jay had found a place from where they could see everything. As Jay watched Connor calmly guiding Abby from one hold to the next, he wondered how he could have got Connor so completely wrong. It looked like Toby had been right about him all along. He didn't seem stuck up or annoying now. Jay knew that they'd be in serious trouble without him. All the others trusted him – Jay could see that. *And I trust him too*, he thought, astonished at himself.

'They've done it!' said Priya suddenly. 'Look! Abby's climbing on her own.'

Moments later they saw that Connor and Abby had reached the foot of the cliff.

'But what's Connor doing now?' asked Jay. Connor had taken the rope off Priya and was climbing swiftly back towards Toby. 'He can't just leave her down there.'

Connor had reached Toby now. He put the rope over his shoulders, and after a few quick words with Toby, he began to climb back up to the top. Toby followed him as far as the ledge with the little tree.

'Quick,' Connor said, his head appearing over the edge a surprisingly short time later. 'Put everything back in Toby's rucksack and bring it over here. In fact, you might as well bring them all.'

'But why?' asked Jay, his heart beating faster. 'What are we going to do?'

'Abby can't come up,' Connor said. 'So we all have to go down.'

Jay looked at the ground and felt himself turning pale. 'I've never done anything like that,' he said.

'It's not a hard climb,' Connor told him as Priya and Andy brought the rucksacks over. 'Now I've been down I can see how to do it. Once you get to the ledge where Toby is, you can climb the rest of the way quite easily. In fact, the whole thing is simple once you know where the holds are. But let's lower these bags down first and get Abby warm.'

Working quickly, Connor looped the rope through the rucksack handles and lowered them as far as the ledge where Toby was waiting before climbing down to join him. They sent the bags on down to the bottom and Connor followed. Andy had left his perch on the ledge now and was working his way back to join Jay and Priya. Jay watched Connor pulling things out of Toby's rucksack and pouring Abby a drink from the flask. He wrapped Abby in a foil blanket, then untied the rope, coiled it around his shoulders, and climbed quickly up past Toby to the top once more.

'You see?' he said to Jay, breathing hard with

the effort of the climb. 'It's not as bad as it looks
. . . You can go next, Andy.' He fastened the rope
around Andy's waist.

'It's only the first bit that's scary,' Toby called
up. 'Just dangle your legs over the edge and you'll
find a place to put your feet. After that it's easy.'

Jay watched anxiously as Andy climbed down.
Very soon now, he was going to have to do the
same. And he wasn't sure he could. He forced
himself to watch. Andy had reached Toby on the
ledge. He took off the rope and scrambled easily
the rest of the way to join Abby at the bottom.

'OK, Priya,' Connor said, fastening the rope
once more. 'Are you ready? It really is much
easier than it looks from up here. I'll climb down
in front of you to show you where to go.'

Priya hesitated. 'I don't understand,' she said,
looking nervously at the small figures of Andy
and Abby sitting on the rocks below. 'If it's so
easy, why did Abby get stuck?'

'It happens,' Connor told her. 'It can even
happen to the best rock climbers. You just

suddenly feel really exposed. But it's best not to talk about it now – OK? Let's just do it.'

He let himself over the edge and guided Priya's feet to the first ledge. 'See?' he said. 'There's nothing to it.'

When Priya was halfway down, Jay sent the rope after her and Toby paid out the rope as Connor helped her to climb to the bottom.

Jay waited at the edge of the cliff. It was crazy. He shouldn't be feeling scared like this. If Priya could do it without any fuss, then he could too. And he hated the idea of Connor and Toby having to climb all the way back up just to help him down.

'Hey, Connor,' he called. 'I'm sure I can do it on my own. You don't have to come back up.'

'No way,' Connor shouted urgently. 'Stay where you are.'

He climbed rapidly back to the top. Toby followed more slowly.

'Sorry, Jay,' said Connor seriously, then paused to catch his breath. 'You haven't done this before. It's better to be safe. You wait until you go over the edge and you'll see why.'

All the good things Jay had been thinking about Connor vanished in an instant and he turned to say something. Connor was doing it again, treating him like a kid.

But Toby was there beside him. 'Here, put this around you,' he said. 'Now, over there.'

Before he knew it, Jay was over the edge of the cliff and Connor was guiding him downwards as Toby paid out the rope from above. 'Bring your left foot down here,' Connor said. 'There's a sticking-out bit of rock.'

Jay looked down between his legs and the world seemed to spin. He put his foot quickly back where it had been a moment before, and held onto the rock tightly. 'You're OK,' said Connor, and Jay knew that he had sensed his panic.

'Don't look down,' Connor told him. 'It makes everything seem worse. Ready? Now move your foot.'

Jay was suddenly glad that he hadn't snapped at Connor a few moments earlier, because Connor had been dead right. If he'd been climbing down alone, what would have happened? The same as had happened to Abby, he supposed. He followed Connor's instructions gratefully, and when they were halfway down they rested on the ledge.

'OK, Toby,' Connor yelled.

The rope came slithering over the rocks, and Connor gathered it in. 'But how's Toby going to get down?' asked Jay.

'Like this,' said Toby, arriving on the ledge beside them.

'But you climbed down that without a rope.'

'I'd already climbed *up* it without a rope,' Toby said. 'Or hadn't you noticed?' He grinned. 'And it really isn't that hard. Not once you know how.'

Jay shook his head. It seemed that Toby was a lot tougher than he'd ever imagined.

'Come on,' Toby said. 'Don't stand there staring. Let's get to the bottom.'

And just a couple of minutes later the three boys had reached the foot of the cliff.

'OK,' Connor said, turning to Abby, Andy and Priya – but he stopped with his mouth open. They had vanished. 'I don't believe it,' he said. 'What have they done now?'

'Look,' said Toby. 'They're down there.'

Abby appeared between two trees, running towards them. 'It's OK,' she shouted breathlessly. 'There's a path. People come here. We found footprints and a chocolate wrapper. Look! Come on, Connor, you might look pleased.'

'You went off on your own again,' he said, frowning.

'You don't understand,' said Andy, coming up beside Abby with Priya behind him. 'It wasn't dangerous. It's like a proper path. People must come this way to visit the waterfall.'

'No, Connor's right,' said Priya. 'We should have waited. I just wanted to explore,' she explained to him. 'And Abby was feeling loads better, and we only went a little way. And it really is a path.'

Connor shook his head. 'You're all crazy,' he muttered. Abby was amazing. Ten minutes earlier she'd been pale and shivering, and now she seemed to be ready for anything again. 'At least we're all safe,' he said. 'And if you're right, then we should be able to get back soon. Have you got the map, Toby? How far is it?'

The waterfall was clearly marked on the map in blue letters and so, now that they studied it, was the footpath. 'It's about three kilometres,' said Toby, looking up. 'If we get a move on, we could be back in half an hour. And with any luck we'll have a phone signal before then.'

'Well, we haven't got one now,' Connor said grimly. 'The event was due to end at two p.m. It's nearly four o'clock now. Rick's probably already started a search. It won't matter how fast we get back – we're still going to be in a whole lot of trouble. He's bound to have called the police by now.'

CHAPTER 16

'Is everybody ready to go?' Connor asked.

'Hang on,' said Toby, fiddling with his rucksack. 'I've got some emergency rations that I haven't used.' He pulled out half a dozen bars of chocolate and handed them round. 'I think we deserve them,' he told the others. 'I mean – look. We've just climbed down there . . .'

Unwrapping their chocolate, the team turned back for a moment. Andy had his camcorder out again. He panned from Toby's serious face to the scene in front of them. The walls of the gorge rose sharply on both banks of the stream, birch and red-berried rowan trees clinging to the sides. The black face of the cliff blocked off the end of the valley, the waterfall plummeting down in a ribbon of white spray. It looked steep and very dangerous.

'Come on,' said Connor with a shudder. 'Let's get out of here.' It had been a difficult decision, bringing them all down the cliff. He and Toby had both known that it would mean climbing without a rope, but Toby hadn't hesitated. Connor was very glad that he was his APL.

The path zigzagged rapidly downhill, keeping close to the banks of the tumbling stream, and Connor led them at a good pace, checking from time to time that they were all keeping up. Every few minutes he looked at his phone anxiously. He was dreading making the call, but he was also worried that with every minute that passed, more and more people might be starting to look for them. He thought of Rick, phoning all their parents, and wondered what he was going to say to him when they finally got back – and to his dad.

Ten minutes later the stream emerged from the rocky gorge and turned to the right. Ahead of them they saw a track and a fence, and beyond the fence the fields rolled away towards a distant town. The dark clouds were starting to break up and a sudden gleam of orange sunlight lit up the landscape.

'We have to really hurry now,' Connor said. 'It'll be starting to get dark soon. How about trying to jog along the track for a bit?'

They all nodded their agreement, but then Connor glanced at the phone. 'There's a signal!' he said. 'No – it's gone again.' He paused, and then shook his head. 'I'm sure it was there. Maybe we should wait a bit and see if it comes back.'

'We can get to the car park in twenty minutes,' Toby replied. 'And the chances are we'll meet someone out looking for us . . . They're going to be angry, aren't they,' he added nervously.

'They'll be pleased we're alive,' Abby said. '*Then* they'll be angry. Come on, let's get moving. The longer we wait, the worse it'll be.'

They jogged along the rough track for another ten minutes, each lost in thought. The cries of birds came from the moors on their right, where the sky was now clear and bright. On their left the fields gave way to wood, and below them they caught occasional glimpses of the stream they had followed from its moorland source.

Suddenly Connor stopped.

'Hey!' yelped Abby, bumping into the back of him. 'What are you doing?'

'I thought I heard something,' he said.

'It was birds,' said Andy. 'Curlews, I think, up on the moors.'

'No, listen – there it is again.'

This time they all heard it – a sharp cry of pain from somewhere off to their right.

'There's a path,' Priya said. 'Over here. Come on.'

They all followed her. The path led to a kind of hollow in the hillside, overhung with trees and criss-crossed with tracks and humps. In front of them they saw three bikes abandoned on the ground, and beside them lay a boy. Another boy and a girl were bending over him, but they looked up when they heard footsteps, and Connor stared at them in astonishment. He'd last seen them jeering at them as the minibus pulled out of the car park at Scout HQ.

'Forget it,' said Jay. 'Let's go.'

'We can't,' said Connor. 'Look – he's hurt.'

Jay stared at the boy on the ground. It was Sean, and he was moaning with pain. Jay couldn't believe that the gang had followed them all the way out here. 'He's most likely pretending,' he said bitterly.

'We have to get to the car park,' Toby said. 'Why don't we carry on? Then we can send somebody back to help them.'

'Don't go,' Vicky pleaded, and Jay saw that her face was streaked with dirt and tears. Lee looked at the ground and said nothing. 'Please, you have to help,' she went on. 'Sean fell off his bike and he's done something to his arm.'

'Yeah, and I bet it was his own fault too,' Jay said.

'We have to be sure,' said Connor. 'He might be badly hurt. Even if we get help, whoever comes will need to know about his injuries. I'll be as quick as I can.'

He put his rucksack down and went over to Sean. 'Where does it hurt?' he asked, but Sean just let out another moan and didn't reply.

Jay turned on Vicky. 'What were you doing here?' he demanded.

'We came up here to ride our bikes,' replied Vicky sulkily. 'There's no law against that, is there?'

Jay looked at the bikes and laughed. They were a mess. The chains and cables were rusty and the tyres had splits and cracks in them. And he knew that none of them were the slightest bit interested in mountain biking. He knew because they'd laughed at him once when he'd suggested trying it. It was hard to believe that he'd ever imagined they were his friends. 'Right, so you didn't follow us up here so you could cause trouble?'

'Jay, leave it,' Toby muttered, looking at Vicky. 'I think you ought to sit down – you've had a shock,' he told her.

'He's right,' said Abby, handing her a tissue. 'Come over here.' She took Vicky's arm and led her across to a fallen tree trunk. Priya went with them.

Jay thought Abby was amazing. She'd had a terrible time on the cliff, but she seemed to have recovered completely, and now she was looking after someone else.

'How did it happen?' Connor called over to Vicky. Lee was standing on one side and wouldn't even look at them. 'Did he just fall off? Did he bang his head?'

'We were just riding around,' said Vicky, blowing her nose on a tissue that Priya had given her. 'We were going over these humps and things, and Sean decided to go from up there.' She pointed to a path that ran almost vertically up the side of the hollow.

'Why would he do that?' asked Andy. 'It's crazy.'

'He wanted to get air,' Lee explained, suddenly talkative. 'You know, like, take off and stuff.'

'Only he came down too fast,' continued Vicky. 'And his brakes don't work very well. He went up in the air all right but he sort of twisted and came down with the bike on top of him.'

Jay looked at the mangled bike, and then glanced up at the slope. He shuddered. Doing something like that without a helmet was just stupid. Sean was lucky he hadn't knocked himself out – or worse.

'It's my arm,' said Sean, through gritted teeth. 'I put it down to try and stop myself. There was a sort of weird noise. I think I might have broken it.' He was lying on his side, the injured arm folded at an odd angle beneath him.

'Did you bang your head?' Connor asked.

'No,' replied Sean. 'I told you. It's my arm.'

'And can you move everything? Can you move your feet?'

Sean hesitated. 'Yes,' he said after a moment. 'My leg hurts where the bike banged down on me, but it's not as bad as my arm. Why do you keep asking me all these questions? I—'

Before Connor could stop him, Sean rolled over onto his back. He screamed with pain, and then turned even whiter than he'd been before.

'You're cold,' said Connor suddenly. 'How long has he been lying here?' he asked the others.

'I'm not sure,' Vicky replied. 'Fifteen minutes? Maybe longer. We didn't know what to do. There's no phone signal.'

'We need to get him back to the car park as fast as we can,' said Connor.

Jay could see that he was really worried now. Suddenly there was no question of them leaving Sean behind. He would have to come with them. Jay remembered something from the first-aid session earlier in the term. 'Is it safe to move him?' he asked.

'I don't think you're supposed to move someone who might have broken something, but he's really cold,' Connor said. 'And I'm as sure as

I can be that it's just his arm that he's hurt. We'll need that foil blanket, Toby. Who's got the first-aid kit?'

'Me,' said Jay. He took off his rucksack and began to unpack it.

'I'll need the big triangular bandage,' Connor told him.

Jay found that his fingers wouldn't do what he wanted. He pulled things out of his rucksack and fumbled with the zip on the first-aid kit. 'Is this it?' he asked, pulling out a white rectangular package. He turned it round and saw from the label that it was the bandage Connor was looking for. He started to tear open the plastic package.

'Great,' said Connor. 'Can you sit up?' he asked Sean. 'If you can do it on your own, then you probably haven't hurt anything else too badly.'

Jay couldn't believe that Connor was being so calm. Every minute they spent helping Sean was making things worse for all of them, but it seemed almost as if Connor had forgotten all that. Sean put his good arm on the ground and pushed himself upright. He moaned slightly as he sat up, and held his injured arm.

'How does it feel?' Connor asked.

'It's OK as long as I don't move it,' Sean said. He touched the middle of his forearm. 'This bit feels weird. Ouch!'

'OK,' said Connor. 'We'll try and fix your arm just like that. Keep holding it while I tie the bandage.'

Jay passed the bandage to Connor and watched admiringly as he deftly passed one end under Sean's arms and then took the other end up around his neck. He tied a reef knot. 'There, now pull your good arm out really carefully. How does that feel?'

Sean winced as he pulled the arm out, leaving the sling holding his injured arm firmly in place. He nodded. 'It's not too bad, thanks.'

'That was cool,' said Andy, lowering his camcorder. 'Absolutely perfect.'

'Hey!' said Lee. 'Don't point that thing at me.'

Andy shrugged and aimed the camera instead at the fallen tree, where Priya and Abby were sitting with Vicky.

'Have you done it?' asked Priya. 'Can we go?'

Connor nodded as Toby wrapped the foil blanket around Sean. 'Let's get moving,' he said.

'I'll bring his bike,' said Jay, putting on his rucksack.

He picked up the bike and saw that the wheel was shaped like a banana. There was no way he could push it. Then he remembered a trick he'd seen a man in the bike shop do. He laid the bike down. The opposite edges of the buckled wheel curved into the air. Jay placed a foot on one edge, pushing it down until it was in contact with the ground, then put his other foot on the opposite edge and gave a little jump, transferring all his weight onto the rim. He felt the wheel give, and when he picked the bike up again, the wheel was almost true. He gave it an experimental spin. It caught a little on the brakes, but it was good enough. He looked up and saw that the others were all staring at him.

'That's the most surprising thing I've seen all day,' Connor said.

'I know,' said Andy. 'And I got it on camera too.'

'It's just a trick,' Jay said. But he couldn't help feeling pleased.

They walked slowly back along the track, Connor supporting Sean. He was very weak, and it seemed to take for ever to walk the final kilometre, but finally they turned a corner and Jay saw the car park ahead of them. The minibuses had gone, and the trees were lit eerily by the flashing blue lights of a police car and van. Seconds later they heard the sound of voices.

Jay looked at Connor. 'Don't worry,' he said. 'I told you I'd make sure they know it wasn't your fault, and that's what I'll do.'

Connor paused. 'Thanks, Jay – I—'

But before he could say any more they heard shouts from the car park and saw two tall figures silhouetted against the flashing lights.

'They've seen us,' said Toby. 'Come on, let's get it over with.'

Rick and Connor's dad came running towards them, followed by several police officers. As they got closer, Jay saw that a small crowd of people were gathered in the car park.

'Thank God!' exclaimed Rick. 'You're all safe! Let me count you to make sure . . . five . . . six . . . seven. But there are nine of you. And bikes too . . .'

'Whatever have you been doing?' asked Dr Sutcliff. 'Have you any idea how worried we've been?'

'Please, Dad,' said Connor. 'Before you ask us anything else, could you look at Sean? I think he's broken his arm, and he's very cold. I'm pretty sure he needs to go to hospital.'

'Are you sure *you're* OK?' asked his dad anxiously. 'Grandpa and Grandma came up to see you finish. They didn't know what to think. Neither did I.'

'Don't be daft,' said Connor's grandpa, coming up behind them. 'I wasn't worried. Connor's got the famous knife, hasn't he? It's our lucky mascot, that knife is. I knew they'd be all right.'

Jay looked at Connor's grandpa and saw that his face was pale, his eyes searching anxiously to check that Connor and the rest of them were safe. Suddenly Jay felt shaky. He knew it wasn't going to be easy to explain what had happened.

Connor's dad knelt down beside Sean, who had slumped to the ground. 'Let's take a look,' he said. 'Who fixed this sling?'

'It was Connor,' answered Jay.

'Hmmm. Well, you've done one thing right, at least,' said a police officer.

'He's broken his arm,' Dr Sutcliff said, looking up. 'It's immobilized nicely, so I don't think you need to call an ambulance. You can take him in the car.'

'Let's get you sat down with some tea before

we talk,' said Rick, beckoning Tiger Patrol towards him. 'You know, we were about to call out half the county's police and the Search and Rescue team. You're only just in time.'

CHAPTER 17

Most of the helpers from the Orienteering Club had stayed on, ready to mount a search for the missing Scouts, but once they knew Tiger Patrol were safe, they climbed into their cars and left. At the side of the car park, Rick boiled water on a gas stove and made them all mugs of hot, sweet tea. They watched as one of the police cars departed with Sean, Lee and Vicky. To Jay's surprise, Vicky gave a little wave as they drove past, her face pale and worried. Once Connor's grandma had checked for herself that he was all in one piece, she and his grandpa left too.

Jay turned back and saw Rick surveying them grimly. 'Well, then,' Rick said. 'You'd better tell me what happened.'

Until now none of them had said a thing,

but suddenly they were all talking at once. 'We got lost.'

'The woods went on for ever.'

'The clouds came down and we didn't know which stream was which.'

'It wasn't Connor's fault.'

Rick held up both hands. 'Let's just start at the beginning,' he said. 'And I'd like to hear it from the Patrol Leader, if you don't mind.'

'But it was me,' said Jay, ignoring him. 'I was angry and I ran off, and they came and found me. It was *good* what they all did. They didn't do anything wrong. If they'd just left me on my own, I'd never have found my way back.'

Rick looked at him, and Jay returned his searching gaze. He felt himself flushing, but he wasn't going to let the others take the blame for his mistake.

Rick turned to Connor. 'You had very clear instructions,' he said. 'If a member of your patrol was lost or injured, you were to go to the next control point and fetch help. You all knew that, didn't you?'

They all hung their heads. 'It was my decision,' Connor said. 'After last time I wanted to show you we could do it right. We thought we'd be able to find Jay and get back on course and no one would know. It was stupid.'

'And Connor didn't really want to do it, either,' said Priya, 'whatever he says. It was us who wanted to go after Jay. All of us. Wasn't it?' she demanded, looking at the others.

'It's true,' said Toby.

'There are some things I don't understand here,' Rick said. 'First of all, why did you run off in the first place, Jay? It was an incredibly silly thing to do, but something must have happened to make you do it. And when you lot went after him, how come you couldn't find your way back? How far did you go, for goodness' sake?'

'It was because of me,' said Connor, looking him in the eye. There was a chorus of disagreement from the others, but he went on, 'I was angry. That's why Jay ran off. He'd been walking really slowly and I thought we'd never win like that and I lost my temper. I'm sorry.'

They were all silent for a moment. Jay glanced over at Connor's dad, who was standing nearby, listening. It didn't seem fair that Connor was getting into trouble like this – that they all were. If it hadn't been for him running away, none of this would have happened. But Rick was talking again.

'So you all followed Jay,' he said. 'Where did you go?'

'That's where it really went wrong,' said Andy. 'We all knew we weren't supposed to cross the track, but we didn't even think about it.'

'And none of us checked which direction we were going,' said Toby glumly.

'Or how long we'd been walking,' put in Abby. 'When we finally found Jay, we realized that we didn't know where we were.'

'Or how to get back,' said Priya.

Rick shook his head. 'I'm hoping that

somewhere along the line you did *something* sensible,' he said. 'Or did you just find your way back by accident?'

'It was Andy who worked out what to do,' Connor said. 'And Abby too. Oh, and it was Toby who had the Ordnance Survey map in his rucksack.'

He explained how they had found their way out of the woods and onto the moors. 'At least we knew which woods we were in,' he said. 'And when we didn't find the track, we knew we were too far north, so we headed across the moor and aimed to hit the streams. It was Jay who worked it out.'

'You weren't scared?' asked Rick in surprise. 'Walking across the moors in that weather? I don't suppose you could see very far.'

'Connor and Toby knew what to do,' said Priya. 'It was nasty up there, and I was really frightened, but they were very careful. And Jay too. And we did find the stream.'

'Only we weren't completely sure which one

it was,' continued Connor. 'We talked about it, and we decided we had to get off the moors as quickly as we could, even if we had a long way to walk at the end. We did keep trying to call you, but there was never a signal.'

'And then we got to the waterfall,' said Toby. 'We stayed close to the stream and the valley turned into a gorge.'

'OK,' said Rick. 'So you turned back and worked your way over the hill. That was sensible.'

'Well, no,' said Connor. 'We—'

'It was me,' Abby interrupted. 'You can't blame Connor. He was amazing. If he hadn't—'

'What are you saying, Abby? What happened?' Jay heard a tremor in Rick's voice. He looked at him, and even in the fading light he was sure that Rick's brown face had gone pale.

'I tried to climb down the cliff,' Abby said faintly. 'And . . . and I got stuck. I thought . . . I thought I was going to fall.' Jay heard her catch her breath.

'Oh, Abby,' said Rick quietly, and Jay knew

that he was picturing in his mind what might have happened. Suddenly Jay had a vision of how Rick must be seeing this, and he realized for the first time just how much danger they had been in.

'It looked easy,' said Abby. 'I mean, it *was* easy really. Only halfway down I just panicked.'

'I climbed down to her,' Connor continued. 'Toby had a rope in his rucksack—'

'A rope!' exclaimed Rick. 'Why on earth did you think you'd need a rope on an orienteering exercise?'

'Well, I didn't,' said Toby. 'Not really. It just seemed a useful kind of thing to take.'

For the first time, Rick smiled. 'Just as well you did,' he said. 'So how did you get Abby up again?'

'We didn't,' Connor said, and he explained the whole rescue to Rick. 'I thought we shouldn't split up,' he said. 'And that meant we all had to go down to Abby. It was safe enough, once we'd climbed it once.'

'Without proper equipment,' Rick muttered

almost to himself, 'and with kids who'd never been on rocks before. When I think about what might have happened . . .'

'We were as careful as we could be,' Toby said. 'Connor made everyone move away from the bottom of the cliff while we were climbing. And we used the rope as much as we could.'

'*As much as you could!* Exactly, Toby. For at least some of the time some of you were clambering around on a cliff face without any protection at all.' Rick paused, then smiled ruefully. 'I suppose it could have been a whole lot worse. In fact, I'd say you did very well in the circumstances. You had to make some difficult decisions, but it sounds as if you all worked together and made the best of a bad situation. It's just a pity you got yourselves into the situation in the first place.'

'It's all right, Rick,' said Connor stiffly. 'You don't have to say it. I'll resign as Patrol Leader. Anyone can see that Toby would do a much better job than me.'

Connor's dad put a hand on his shoulder. 'Connor, you don't have to—'

'I messed up, Dad, you know I did. I—'

Rick held up a hand. 'What do the rest of you think?' he asked.

'Connor didn't mess up at all,' Jay burst out hotly. 'He was brilliant. I could never have climbed down that cliff if he hadn't shown me how to do it. And it was amazing how he got Abby to start climbing again. He got everyone down safely.'

'Jay's right,' said Toby. 'Connor worked out what to do and he did it really fast. And I bet if I hadn't had the rope he'd have done it anyway.'

'I couldn't have hung on much longer,' Abby said.

'None of us could have done what Connor did,' added Andy. 'I was watching him all the time.'

'You see?' Rick said to Connor. 'It looks as if you didn't do quite as badly as you think you did.'

'And it was fair enough, Connor getting angry

with me,' Jay put in. 'I was being a pain in the neck.'

The others all laughed. 'That's definitely true,' said Priya.

'But it wasn't OK, though, was it?' Connor said, ignoring their laughter. 'That was the worst thing of all. I should have known.'

'But you know now, don't you?' said his dad quietly.

Connor nodded.

'You brought your patrol home safely,' said Rick. 'That's the most important thing. And a very good patrol they are too.'

The Tigers looked at each other.

Rick turned to Connor again. 'Everyone in your patrol thinks you did a good job, and that's good enough for me, Connor.'

'It's good enough for me too,' said Connor's dad. 'I reckon your grandpa's going to love hearing what happened. It's about time you had some stories of your own to tell.'

He put his arm around Connor and gave him

a hug, and Connor felt his eyes stinging with tears. He blinked and rubbed them away.

'You're all exhausted right now,' said Rick as the patrol car that had taken the gang to the hospital swung into the car park again and the two officers got out. 'You made some bad mistakes today,' he continued, 'but you sorted yourselves out and made it back safely. Well done, all of you. And that includes you, Jay. Don't you even think about leaving the Scouts!'

Jay flushed. The others were all nodding and smiling at him. 'OK,' he said. 'I'll stay. But only if Connor says he'll still be Patrol Leader.'

'Connor?' said a young woman police officer. 'Are you the boy who put that young man's arm in a sling?'

Connor nodded. 'Is he all right?' he asked anxiously. 'I mean, I didn't like to move him, but he was so cold, and I didn't know how long it would be before he got help if we left him, and—'

The officer stopped him. 'He's fine. They said

at the hospital that it was a nasty break. He was in shock and he wasn't exactly dressed for a day out on the moors. Any longer out here and hypothermia would have set in. You did all the right things. Well done, Connor. Good job, all of you. And now, let's get you home.'

They piled wearily into the back of the police van. Connor and his dad were the last, and as Connor was about to climb in, Dr Sutcliff put a hand on his shoulder.

'Hey, Connor,' he whispered in his ear. 'I'm proud of you.'

CHAPTER 18

The following day was Sunday, and Jay astonished his mum by sleeping most of the morning. 'Well,' she said when he appeared for breakfast at lunch time, 'I'm glad you've been out having adventures instead of playing on that computer all day, but it's lucky you don't have school tomorrow. I hope Scouts isn't always going to be as tiring as this.'

Jay grinned. 'I hope so too. Did you tell the neighbours I hadn't been arrested?'

When he arrived home in the police van the night before, people had been peering from windows all along the street.

'Of course I did!' said his mum. 'They were saying all sorts of things. Couldn't you have got the police to drop you at the end of the street?'

247

Before Jay could answer there was a knock on the door. His mum returned with Toby.

'We're all meeting up at Andy's house,' Toby said. 'He's made a movie of our expedition. Him and Connor have been working on it all morning. He's planning to show it at our next meeting but he wants us all to see it first.'

Jay felt himself flushing. He wasn't exactly going to look good in the movie.

'Oh, that's nice,' said his mum, to make things worse. 'I'd like to see it too.'

'I told you, Mum,' said Jay. 'We did lots of things wrong.'

'But that nice man who came back with you – Chris, wasn't it? Connor's dad? He said you all did very well. And he's a doctor, so he should know.'

'Don't worry,' said Toby, looking at Jay. 'That's why we're going round. To make sure Andy hasn't made us look like idiots. He wouldn't, you know.'

Jay felt a little better, but he couldn't help

worrying. Last night, on the way back, Rick had said that it would be good if they could talk to the whole troop about what had happened to them. That would have been bad enough, but a movie . . . It was hard to see how Andy could avoid making him look stupid.

'Well, really,' said his mum as there was another knock at the door. 'It's like Piccadilly Circus in here today.'

Jay heard the door open and then his mum's voice. The door closed with a bang.

'The cheek!' his mum said, coming back into the room. 'That girl is nothing but trouble, and now she comes knocking on our door. How dare she!'

'But who was it?' asked Jay. 'What did they want?'

'She wanted to talk to you,' his mum replied. 'It was that girl who hangs out on the corner. Vicky – that's her name— Jay? Where are you going?'

Jay pushed past her and ran to the door. Toby

followed him. 'Wait!' called Jay. 'Is Sean OK?'

Vicky stopped on the pavement and turned round. 'They kept him in hospital,' she said. 'They had to do an operation on his arm. But he's going to be all right. I came to . . . Well, you know, I came to say thanks. Tell your friend, will you? The one who helped him.'

'Right,' said Jay awkwardly. 'Well, I'm glad he's OK.'

Toby nodded. They waited. Vicky seemed as if she was about to say something else, but then a shout came from the end of the street, and they saw Lee standing there.

'Come on, Vick,' he yelled. 'What do you want to talk to that lot for?'

Vicky shrugged, and ran off down the street. She said something to Lee, then the two of them laughed and walked away.

Jay and Toby found the rest of Tiger Patrol clustered around the computer in Andy's living room.

'Great!' said Andy. 'I've just finished editing it. Take a look.'

The film began with shots of all the members of Tiger Patrol. There were Andy and Abby, both pulling faces at the camera. Then there were shots of Jay and Priya on their first day in their new uniforms, and one of Toby with his enormous rucksack. Finally they saw Connor looking at a map and then pointing across the moors. Then the titles flashed onto the screen. TIGER PATROL IN CLIFF RESCUE. In smaller letters Andy had inserted: *How not to go orienteering!*

Jay felt a little sick as the film cut to a shot of the Tigers walking across the moor towards the first control point. He saw himself walking a long way behind, dragging his feet, but then he heard Connor's voice on the movie saying: 'You should always travel at the speed of the slowest member of the party. If you don't, you might get separated.'

The next sequence showed the patrol making their way through the marshy grassland, and now

Connor's voice was saying: 'If one of your party gets lost, don't panic like we did. Make sure you keep track of where you're going.'

Jay glanced at Andy, who grinned back at him. 'Well, Rick didn't say we had to tell them *everything*,' he said. 'I mean, they all know we made mistakes, but this is supposed to show how to get out of a bad situation. Look – we're in the woods now. This is where it starts to get good . . .'

The Scout HQ rang with applause and yells. It was the first meeting after half term, and Andy's film had just come to an end.

'Well done, Andy,' Rick said, stepping forward. 'You had some really exciting footage in that movie – much *too* exciting as far as I'm concerned. Andy's managed to make a great movie out of something that could have been a real disaster,' he told the assembled Scouts, 'so I hope you were all paying attention. We'll be going on night hikes next term, and next summer we'll be going to far wilder country in the north.

The Tigers have just shown you exactly what *not* to do, but they survived.'

'The Survival Squad!' said Julie.

Everyone laughed. 'Luckily,' Rick continued, smiling, 'they gave us a lot of tips on how to act when everything goes wrong. Also, because you Tigers showed excellent navigation skills, and completed a long course on the previous event, we've decided that you should get your Orienteering Badges today with the others. And I have more good news for you. Andy, that film means you've completed your Creative Challenge, so you'll be getting your badge for that tonight.'

There was loud applause, then Rick held up his hands for silence. 'Now, you all saw on Andy's movie how Tiger Patrol stopped and helped those kids. They did all the right things, and thanks to them, Sean, the boy who broke his arm, is making a good recovery. I've got a letter here from his dad, thanking every one of you, Tigers. And, what's more, I've been to the hospital to see

Sean. We had a long chat, and he told me what you all did. You can be very proud of yourselves. Well done, Tigers.'

There was more loud applause. The Tigers found themselves surrounded by the other Scouts, all asking questions.

'The rest of us were all finished by two o'clock,' Sajiv said. 'And then it started to rain and Rick began to get worried. How did you get so lost?'

'It's easier than you think,' said Toby mysteriously.

'But it made a good movie, didn't it?' said Andy.

'It's a pity you didn't film my mum,' Jay commented. 'You should have seen her face. There's me and Rick and a police officer on the doorstep, and a big white police van parked in the street, and all the neighbours looking out of the windows. She was dead worried they'd all think I'd been arrested. And they did too.'

They all laughed. 'Well, I don't think it's fair,'

said Guy. 'You go and get lost and you have a ride home with the police. Nothing that exciting ever happens to me.'

'You should be grateful,' said Rick, joining them. 'We want adventure, not danger, and I rather think that what the Tigers found was danger. Am I right, Connor?'

Connor nodded agreement, suddenly thinking of the moment on the cliff when he'd felt sick and dizzy.

'OK, then,' Rick said. 'It's time for the badge ceremony. Get yourselves ready, everyone.'

Ten minutes later the Scouts emerged into the frosty November night.

'I can't believe I've got my first badge already,' said Priya to Jay excitedly. 'I didn't think we had any chance of getting it.'

'Well, we did,' said Jay, looking pleased. 'And the whole thing was exciting, whatever Rick says. I wonder what's going to be next?'

'Nothing like that,' said Connor. 'We don't

always have adventures getting badges, you know.'

'But we might,' said Andy hopefully, looking at Priya and Abby. 'After all, we're the Survival Squad. You heard Julie.'

'That's right,' said Jay. 'Didn't Rick say we were going on night hikes? Just imagine what might happen!'

'Ghosts!' said Abby.

'Vampires!' laughed Andy.

Suddenly they were all laughing, even Connor. Jay looked around at his new friends. Somehow he had the feeling that Andy was right.

Nothing they did together was ever going to be ordinary.

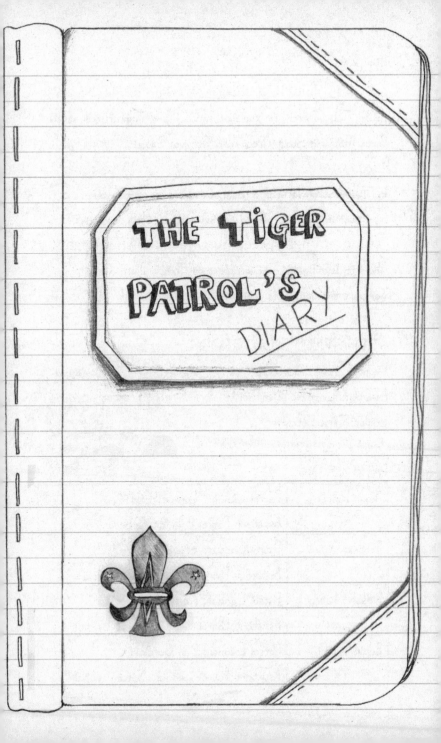

HELLO!

Hi, I'm Toby Church. I'm the new APL of the Tiger Patrol at the Sixth Matfield Scout Troop (aka Survival Squad!).

In Tiger Patrol we keep a notebook where we write down important information. These are some pages from our book.

The 6th Matfield is an average-sized Troop. There are 24 members this year. This is how we're organized.

6TH MATFIELD SCOUT TROOP

Scout Leader: Rick Cole

Assistant Leader: Julie Parfitt

Helper: Chris Sutcliff

PATROLS

Tiger Patrol	Patrol Leader: Connor Sutcliff
	Assistant Patrol Leader: Toby Church
Panther Patrol	Patrol Leader: Sajiv Malik
	Assistant Patrol Leader: Karen Jenkins
Kestrel Patrol	Patrol Leader: Kerry Devlin
	Assistant Patrol Leader: Leroy Lester
Eagle Patrol	Patrol Leader: Ben Garfield
	Assistant Patrol Leader: Sarah Carter

ORIENTEERING Notes from Connor

Orienteering is a cool way to practise navigation skills, especially if you live a long way from wild country. Top orienteers run all the time, but you don't have to do it like that.

THINGS YOU HAVE TO DO TO GET THE BADGE

Know all about the special orienteering maps and symbols. Get the map the right way round and navigate with the map set to the ground. You have to hold the map so that it looks like the area you're facing.

Plot the points you have to navigate to on your own orienteering map. They have a master map at the events and you have to copy from it.

You have to do three orienteering courses. They have different levels of difculty. White is easiest and black is hardest.

You have to learn about safety, first aid, etc., and know the Countryside Code.

HOW TO PACK A RUCKSACK Top tips from Toby

1. Pack light things at the bottom and heavier things at the top.
2. Things you might need quickly should go at the top or in the pockets - e.g. lunch, drink, waterproofs, first-aid kit.
3. Pack things in plastic bags. Use different-coloured bags for different things to help you find them easily.

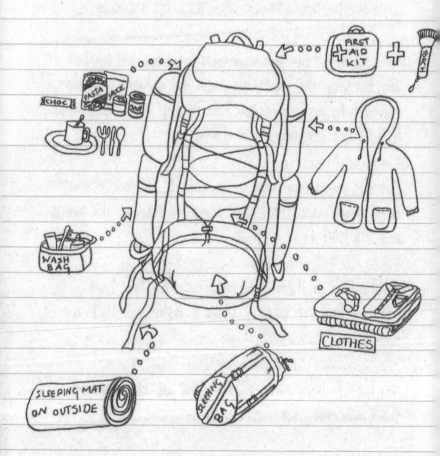

TOP TIPS FOR NAVIGATION Notes from Toby

DON'T FORGET!!!

1. Read the map! Get it the right way round and look at it carefully.

2. Keep track of how long you've been walking. If you know how fast you walk, you can work out roughly how far you've gone. I walk at 5 kph on the pavement and about 4 kph on rough ground. At 4 kph 1 kilometre takes 15 minutes and 100 metres takes 1.5 minutes. It's easy!

3. Orienteering maps are on a VERY large scale. Pay attention to the scale info.

NAVIGATING TO CHANGES OF CONTOURS

When the contours get closer together, the slope gets steeper, and the other way round. This is especially useful in bad weather or snow.

COUNTING STEPS TO ESTIMATE DISTANCE

Everyone's steps are different lengths! You have to check your own.

MY STEPS:

100m (on the flat) = 79 double steps

100m going up London Road (uphill) = 85 double steps

100m going down London Road = 81 double steps

100m across the park (uphill, rough) = 87 double steps

Count double paces, not single (keeps the counting easier!)

NB: Don't try to estimate too much in one go. It's more accurate to walk 100 metres and then stop and check the terrain for the next bit.

NAVIGATING USING TWO COMPASSES Notes from Jay

This is really useful in bad weather.

1. The two people with compasses set the bearing.

2. The leader walks in front following the bearing.

3. Person two (without a compass) follows about 10 metres behind.

4. The third person with a compass follows another 10 metres behind and can easily see if the front two are keeping on course.

5. The leader occasionally looks back, and the person bringing up the rear can point to correct their course.

6. Only give course corrections when the front person looks back (no shouting!)

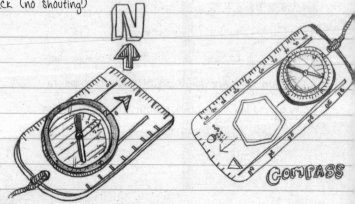

FOOD FOR ORIENTEERING

Notes from Priya

Make sure you have a healthy balanced diet with plenty of fresh fruit and vegetables.

BREAKFAST

Eat a good breakfast in the morning. Oatmeal or porridge is good. Cereal and toast are good too, but lots of sugar isn't. Don't eat too much, especially if you're planning to actually race.

ON THE TRAIL

Take healthy snacks with you, like energy bars and plenty of water. Make sure you remember to drink it!

LUNCH

Don't eat too much lunch. Your digestive system uses energy that you need for orienteering! Too much lunch will slow you down.

Carbohydrates are good: bread, bananas, pasta salad. And you can have a chocolate bar or a piece of cake too.

CONNOR'S GRANDPA'S SURVIVAL CAKE

You need:

150g butter

75g brown sugar

3tbsp honey or golden syrup

250g oats

175g dried fruit

50g nuts, chopped (check if anyone has allergies)

1. Line a 30 x 20cm baking tin with greaseproof paper and grease it.

2. Preheat the oven to 180°C, gas mark 4.

3. Melt butter, sugar and honey/syrup in a pan. Mix everything together, put into the tin and press level with a wooden spoon. Bake until golden (about 20 minutes)

4. Cool for 10 minutes then cut into squares and leave in the tin.

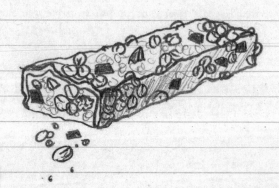

BOWLINE KNOT Abby's notes

It's used to make a loop at the end of a line. Sailors use it a lot, and it used to be the knot most climbers used before they had modern equipment.

It's very secure, but it can work loose if there's no pressure on it.

You make a loop in the standing part, then feed the end up through the loop, around the standing part and back through the loop. There's a story to help you remember it.

The standing part is the tree and the loop is a rabbit hole. The rope end is the rabbit. The rabbit goes up through the hole, round the tree and back down the hole.

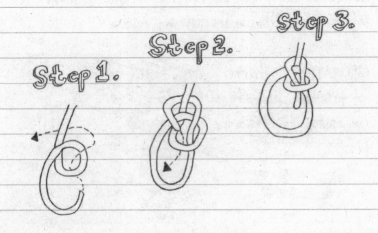

Step 1.   Step 2.   Step 3.

FIRST AID Connor's notes

THINGS TO REMEMBER D R A B C STANDS FOR

DANGER Check for it! It might be an electric cable or there might be rocks about to fall!

RESPONSE Say, 'Can you hear me? Open your eyes.' Shake the injured person's shoulders. If they don't respond they're probably unconscious.

AIRWAY If they are unconscious, then tilt their head back hand on forehead, with two fingers under chin. This should clear the airway.

BREATHING Check for ten seconds — no more! Listen. Watch their chest. See if you can feel their breath. If they're breathing, put them in the Recovery Position.

CIRCULATION If they're not breathing, start CPR 30 compressions to 2 recovery breaths.

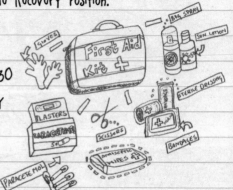

A SLING FOR AN INJURED ARM Connor's notes

1. You need a triangular bandage, or you can use a big scarf, folded to make a triangle.
2. Get the person to hold their injured arm across their chest and keep it still while you work.
3. Put the bandage under their injured arm and around the back of their neck.
4. Put the other part of the bandage over the arm so that the two ends meet at the shoulder. Tie a knot.
5. Tuck the loose ends in at the elbow, or use a pin if you have one.

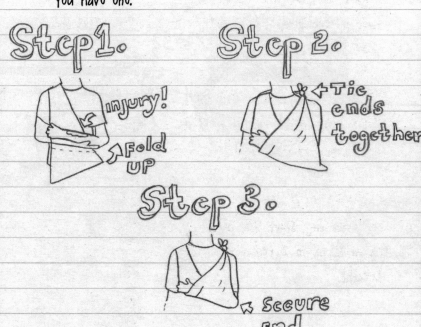

THE CREATIVE CHALLENGE Andy's notes

There are six areas – Performing, Crafts, Promotions, Problem-solving, Construction and Worship – and you have to complete activities from three of them.

I did three main things to get my badge. I performed in a play in my first year in Scouts. Then I took lots of photos at Summer Camp and we used them to make posters to advertise the Scouts. Then I made a film about Orienteering – but I can't tell you any more about that just now!

theatre